After graduating with first cla... Evans entered the accounta... within public practice with on... Specialising in statutory audi... .... ultimately became a director within a small practice before, after more than twenty-five years in accountancy, quitting the profession to care for a parent whose health had deteriorated, and to give more time to those interests and hobbies which had helped render accountancy almost bearable.

The Louise Fawley Symphony is Rikki's first novel, written piecemeal, "late at night, night after night, when all my neighbours were fast asleep, and the only noises were the sounds of the words in my head and the occasional calamitous cat." As literary inspirations, Rikki lists: Dylan Thomas, the arch-druid of poetry in prose; PG Wodehouse, who juxtaposed the serious and the frivolous and bounced the whole comedy along with the skill of a four-piece combo; and Thomas Hardy, that master craftsman of putting a gripping tale on pause to immerse the reader in the sights and sounds of location.

Rikki's interests include all things historical, from castles to candlesticks, music of many genres, from Gregorian Chant to Brit Pop, and above all, like HE Bates, is happiest when working and whiling in a garden.

THE Louise Fawley SYMPHONY

RIKKI EVANS

SilverWood

Published in 2019 by SilverWood Books

SilverWood Books Ltd
14 Small Street, Bristol, BS1 1DE, United Kingdom
www.silverwoodbooks.co.uk

Copyright © Rikki Evans 2019

The right of Rikki Evans to be identified as the author of this work has been asserted in accordance with the Copyright, Designs and Patents Act 1988 Sections 77 and 78.

All rights reserved. No part of this publication may be reproduced, stored in a retrieval system, or transmitted in any form or by any means, electronic, mechanical, photocopying, recording or otherwise, without prior permission of the copyright holder.

This is a work of fiction. Names, characters, places and incidents either are products of the author's imagination or are used fictitiously. Any resemblance to actual events or locales or persons, living or dead, is entirely coincidental.

This book is intended for an adult readership. This story contains scenes of a sexual or challenging nature that some readers may find offensive.

ISBN 978-1-78132-899-6 (paperback)
ISBN 978-1-78132-900-9 (ebook)

British Library Cataloguing in Publication Data
A CIP catalogue record for this book is
available from the British Library

Page design and typesetting by SilverWood Books
Printed on responsibly sourced paper

Acknowledgements

Foremost, my gratitude goes to the team at SilverWood Books who transformed my rough-hewn document into the stunningly-presented volume you see today, and particularly to Helen and Catherine, who led me through the labyrinth of first-time publishing. Also, my special thanks go to Anna, whose enthusiasm for *The Louise Fawley Symphony* turned the task of copy-editing into a joy.

Further, I must thank my friends Nicola, Natacha and Vicki, without whose encouraging words and occasional help, my road to authorship might have been long and rocky indeed. And finally, my heartfelt thanks to my friend Debra, who read 'Melusine' and 'Vetchley' chapter-by-chapter as each rolled off my laptop, and without whose early encouragement the novel easily might have foundered.

First Movement

Melusine

1

NADIR

My life as a EuroScoop Lottery winner had turned out to be dreary and deadly dull. Amid the sparkling champagne euphoria of jackpot joy, the whole of the rest of my life had beckoned in welcome like glorious sunrise after glorious sunrise. But eighteen months on, those spirit-soaring azure-blue skies had clouded to miserable claggy grey. I'd clawed to the bottom of my bucket list and it was empty. Oh, I was bored…so, so bored!

What was the point of my mini mansion with its manicured lawns and prim flowerbeds when there was only me to enjoy them? Where could I dare to push my pedal to the metal in my flash sports car when the roads were littered with speed bumps and cameras? Why hoard wardrobes crammed with gorgeous clothes when there was nobody else to see me in them? I didn't even know the names of the flowers in my garden. I didn't dare go a millimetre an hour over the speed limit with nine points already on my licence. I didn't flaunt my fancy clothes when a whiff of money only attracted every sponger under the sun.

Paris had been clogged with cars and fumes. Venice had been packed with camera-clicking tourists. Rome had been bursting with gorgeous guys, but not one of them had so much as eyed my backside, despite the best efforts of my figure-hugging jeans. Oh, why had I always longed to visit these cities? I'd experienced disappointment after disappointment. I needed something, something else.

It was nearly six months since I'd jettisoned James. The waste of space. I'd imagined that my Big Win would be our happily-ever-after. I'd dreamed of bridal gowns, bedrooms, and babies – three babies at least. But he had seen it as a perpetual season ticket, a lifetime of soccer and rugger matches, as an endless happy hour, pissed-up weekend after pissed-up weekend down the pub with his yobbish, wind-breaking mates. Forgetting my birthday, missing our celebratory meal, and staggering dead-drunk through the door with heaven knows whose knickers atop his head, bawling 'You'll Never Walk Alone' was the last straw. You'll Never Walk Alone? Think again, pal.

Within twenty-four hours I'd thrown a few comfy favourites into the back of my sports car, dumped my cats with my mother, and zoomed off on my continental getaway, determined to reinvent myself. In Milan, I'd ditched my comfy faves for designer glamour. In Vienna, mousey Fawley became blonde bombshell. In Amsterdam, I'd had my lips plumped. Sure, the injections gave me trout pout, but with a dusting of subtly darker skin perfector and a pair of large round shades, back home nobody recognised me. Even my mother and sister had walked by me in the high street. For the first time in my life, I'd felt completely free. Free to be me. Not that odd little girl my mother had brought me up to be, not that gawky young woman she'd grown into. Meet the real Louise Fawley.

I wriggled onto my front. Oh, what to do? When was Jade coming to do my nails? Thursday. Should I call her and see if she could do this afternoon instead? But I fancied that new deep plum colour, and my emerald green would be perfect with the new little dress I'd bought to visit Mother tomorrow.

There was always Plastic Friend…mmm! I felt a first flush of pleasure at the thought. Why not here, on the sun lounger, right in the middle of my lawn? No. That had to be the daftest, most dumb-ass idea I'd ever had. I was already melting in this heat. I didn't want to end up all sweaty and spent. Better save Plastic Friend for later.

I sipped from my glass, more melted ice now than lemonade, wriggled away my bikini-bottom wedgie and grabbed *OMG!* magazine. Inside was a series of adorable pictures of Duchess Charlotte with Prince Peter…what a handsome boy…and what an effortless, natural style Charlotte has…I so admire her, almost in a schoolgirl crush kind of way. No. Nothing like a crush. Not a crush at all. I hastily turned the page.

This was more like it – a page full of pictures of Jon Wetherby, one taken at Twickenham during the Six Nations last spring. What a gorgeous, grinning hunk; a gentleman and a Cambridge scholar too. He could swing low into my sweet chariot anytime. Hmm…what if I could get with him? He must hang out somewhere. My heart leaped at the thought of the caption: "England and Leicester star and Six Nations hero Jon Wetherby pictured with his fiancée, EuroScoop Lottery millionairess Louise Fawley, in a stunning evening gown of her own design." Now that would really piss off James. Maybe I could glean clues where to locate Mr Wetherby. Oh, shit… "Here pictured with fiancée and childhood sweetheart, Joanne Radford, on her father's farm in Lincolnshire." Skinny bitch. Bollocks to Jon Wetherby then. I grumpily turned the page.

What next? "Prince Faisal and Princess Fatima take tea with Richard de Leny, chairman of Melusine Plastics, following the success of this world-beating British family company in winning an £80m order for its heat-resistant drilling components from the Sultanate of Lakash." What? Meanie de Leny taking tea with Faisal and Fatima in his oh-so-eighties beige and brown executive office? My old boss, still in his sickening fawn suit, still drinking from his tacky *Present from Bournemouth* mug? He once gave me a thorough dressing-down in front of my whole accounts team because I'd borrowed his stupid old mug. Meanie de Leny in *OMG!* mag, and me home alone? Oh, this took the flipping biscuit!

I turned onto my back and my eyes filled with hot stinging tears. Not a friend left. Well, okay, one. Helen had grown up with money and had married money; she had no interest in mine. But the others. Scrounging shits. Girls I'd known since St Lucy's. "Oh, we wouldn't ask for ourselves, of course. It's the children. Little Tommy and Johnny love their football but with our washing machine broken I've had to say no this week. They can't play if we've no way of getting their kits clean. But how can you make boys of seven and nine understand? And, oh, we're so tight this month with Dave on short time." So I'd pay for a new washing machine or a new widescreen TV, and the next thing you know they'd be fucking off to Florida for a fortnight, or bombing round the lanes in a gleaming 4x4.

I'd hung my shorts on the back of the lounger, and I reached into the right-hand pocket for Plastic Friend. I needed comforting, cheering, thrilling. How innocent it would look in its pretty pink plastic, more like a child's toy than an adult's. I longed to kiss its end in gentle homage. Instead my hand groped an empty pocket. Dammit. I'd forgotten it. My eyes rose towards my upstairs windows. Oh, what a pain in the arse to have to walk all the way back up to my bedroom. I really just could not be bothered.

Seeing my little loo window slightly ajar presented me with a plan, and my lips parted into a happy, mischievous smile. Of course! I saw at once how I could have some fun and adventure, innocent enough, but at the expense of Meanie de Leny. I'd break into his office in the middle of the night and pinch his poxy mug. I bet he still leaves it cleaned and dried on its coaster ready for the morning. And I'd replace it – my calling card, yes – with a Chokka bar. At Melusine Plastics they'd all called me 'Chokka Cheeks' because I'd always eaten so many. Hey, it was energy food. Oh, this was the perfect crime – one that does nobody any real harm.

I leaped up, grabbed my shorts, *OMG!* mag, and lemonade, and then strode smugly, still smirking, into my kitchen. The microwave clock showed 15:52. I'd shower, heat up a pizza, think through my plan, and grab a few hours' sleep. Then, a swift sixty-mile drive would take me to Melusine Plastics. Oh, this was going to be fun!

2

Night Rider

Check me out! I looked so SAS! I eyed my reflection once more for luck. I'd ferreted out an old black woolly balaclava James had worn for a paintballing weekend, and now sported it with a tight-fitting black fleece jacket that stretched down to my black Lycra leggings. I completed my camouflage with black gloves, black socks, black pumps. My pumps didn't quite look right but my black trainers stank and my army of black boots were all too heavy for what I had in mind, so black pumps it had to be. Since I'd returned from the Continent, I'd gravitated away from my designer dalliance towards high-end high street, but I'd still struggled to dress combat-ready.

Funny how an inconspicuous item of clothing can spark off nostalgia – I could still smell James on his balaclava (he'd obviously put it away dirty – typical), and, strangely, wearing something of his made me feel somehow safe, secure. Those paintballing adventures had invoked an almost animal spirit in James, and to my delicious delight he'd pumped that primal aggression right onto my sweet spot night after night for a week. At my bleary-eyed desk I'd assured the girls that paintballing was the secret ingredient for a lifetime of happy lovemaking. Oh, James. Why did you go and turn into a total arse?

My slimline fleece exaggerated my hips, making my bum look round and large, but if all went according to plan, no one would be giving my arse a second glance anyway. I gave myself a generous smile in the mirror. I was ready. I grabbed a Chokka bar from my bedside stash (no, make that two, three, five; I'd need an energy boost), my car keys and my credit cards. Time to go, Fawley. Let Operation Meanie commence!

I'd chosen to take my little black Mondiale 500 – I'd fancied it would be less conspicuous – and Gwynfor had left it by my front door as requested. He'd also slooshed it clean, which I hadn't wanted (I always think a grubby car draws less attention than a gleaming one), and, I discovered on turning the key, he'd forgotten to fill her up, which I had wanted. Luckily there was still plenty of petrol. The tiny engine coughed into life, the headlights flooded my gravel drive with their luminous beams, and we were away, I in my cute Cinq Cent, pausing only for the obedient electric gates to slowly open and relinquish us out into the night.

A short sprint brought us to the A31 and we headed east, through the bleak, black New Forest. Soon, one by one, road signs to childhood places loomed large from the dark, and my mind drifted back freely to my teenage years. My father had died when I was thirteen, and my life had plummeted. My father had loved his daughters dearly and had treated us equally and fairly, but my mother's long-disguised, polarised attitudes towards my sister and me had suddenly become painfully apparent. I was the tomboy tearaway who needed an unforgiving firm hand; Abigail, the dulcet delight on whose happy lips honey wouldn't melt.

My mother had often threatened me with St Lucy's. When the new school year had started, I'd found myself bussed there, every weekday morning, in putrid, purple uniform, my mother certain that an independent education would prove my salvation. The occasional caning I'd received had been met with complete maternal approval, as proof of added value. Miss Percival! I shuddered, even after all these years. Her dreaded shrine had been a dingy, musty room, where the hapless sacrificial lamb had bent in supplication over an altar-like desk.

I'd barely scraped five GCSEs, all poor passes. Abigail, revelling and basking in the local high school, had cruised to nine the following summer, all As and Bs. Her life became an endless party of Saturday nights in Bournemouth and pony-trekking through the New Forest, accompanied by as many boyfriends as she'd cared to flaunt her cleavage at; mine was unmitigated misery. In the hell of St Lucy's, I was known as Flat Fawley, Poorly Fawley, Crawly Fawley, Mousey Fawley…the girl no boy wanted. When my A-Level grades, as Abigail so kindly pointed out, had spelt D-U-D, my love-six, love-six rout on the sisterly tennis court had seemed complete. I'd had little option but to submissively accept the superiority of my sister and resign myself to my dreary, dead-end life.

Then, something miraculous, truly wonderful, occurred. One slushy, chilly evening, shortly before Christmas, I'd arrived home from my new job as office junior at Melusine Plastics to find Abigail bawling and blubbing like a baby, my mother's comforting arm around her shoulders. What on earth had happened? Oh, my poor dear sister was pregnant, and in her innocence wasn't really sure who the father was. Naively, she'd confided in her boyfriend, thinking she could depend on him, but instead, he'd dumped her and maliciously spread the news through the entire high school. My spirit suddenly soared with an awakened faith in divine justice. Oh, yes! Oh, yes! Oh, thank you! Oh, thank you! I'd turned away to conceal my joy, not quickly enough, for my mother had hurled a cushion at me and promised that, as old as I was, she'd wipe that smile off my face. Oh, Mother! You couldn't have wiped that smile off my face with a steel scourer.

From that day on, as Abigail's life had slid stage by stage through loneliness, morning sickness, the ordeal of labour, sleepless nights, crappy nappies, depression, so mine had steadily struggled free of the mire. Task by task, day by day, pay packet by pay packet, I'd grafted hard at my little job, gradually winning respect, admiration, friends. Within a year, I'd been promoted to accounts junior, and caught the eye of Giles, the fun, flirtatious sales manager. Our romantic late-night walk after the Christmas party had turned into a snowball fight, into a snowy scrap, into the sweetest of surrenders – I'd delightedly, contentedly discarded my virginity, arse in the air, across a snowman we'd demolished in some prim and proper front garden. I'd moved in with Giles that magical, wonderful-life Christmas Eve…and for the first time in my life, had truly felt not girl, but woman.

Shit, I was already here! Absent-minded, in the reverie of recollection, I'd mistakenly driven up to the factory gates of Melusine Plastics. Deftly, I hauled right down the side alley, my headlights hurtling between red-brick walls, picking out startled stray cats and dodging wheelie bins. My little Cinq Cent then sedately popped out into the quiet, bungalowed cul-de-sac slumbering at the rear of the factory.

There was the empty lay-by. I parked up as planned. Not a sound but my own soft breathing. To my right, across the road, in the blackness lay the rough-grass field where sometimes horses were paddocked, then adjoining, the first of the tiny, prim 1930s bungalows that led down the hill to the village. To my left, the eight-foot wire mesh perimeter fence of Melusine Plastics, and through the gloom the Administration Block, nestling at the bottom of the lawned bank; by day, populated by chortling, scavenging, crows; by night, patrolled by muscled ex-marine Stuart and snarling Alsatian, Pompey.

My bowels moved a little. Oh, it would be so easy to

set my little 500cc engine purring into life, to scoot down the gentle hill and through the sleepy village to the A31, to slip back home unseen and put the whole silly idea behind me. In just over an hour, I could be curled up in bed with Plastic Friend.

No. Too often I'd wimped out. Not this time. I'd see it through. Time check – 01:03 – perfect. I scoffed a Chokka bar, my tongue scarcely sensing the chocolate, then, silently opening the driver's door and stepping out into the night, stuffed another in my energy-stash leggings pocket to leave on Meanie de Leny's desk. The car door closed with a click. The ghostly, chilly night air clasped me like cold hands gripping my bottom. I shuddered and looked up in awe at that eight-foot fence.

3

Window of Opportunity

I climbed as craftily as a cat, my gloved hands pawing the mesh holes as I scaled the eight-foot fence, the toes of my pumps stealthily supporting my ascent. At the top, I surveyed the scene the best I could through the blackness, here and there the sodium-orange glow of a street lamp aiding my vision, scattered at seemingly random intervals across the factory grounds. Good. The longed-for flash of a torch, denoting the orbit of Stuart and Pompey around the perimeter, flickered on the far side, near the neglected Nature Reserve. It would be at least five minutes before they passed the Admin Block again.

Deftly I descended, my four paws in feline unison,

down, down, inside the factory fence. My trespassing feet touched Melusine Plastics soil again for the first time in, what, nearly eighteen months? Memories cascaded back in the fleeting moonlight. Here, shaded by the pines, we had picnicked and gossiped our lunch breaks away on scorching summer days; there, outside the Marketing Suite, the Christmas tree, resplendent with lights and garlands, would each year magically appear, cheering some damp, drear November evening; there, one hot summer night, Giles and I had…mmm…in my imagination I could still feel those rough bricks against my bare arse as Giles had pinned me to the wall with pulse after pulse of pleasure. Oh, for fuck's sake, Fawley, get a grip. You've got a job to do.

I pattered through the pines to the edge of the VIP car park. As office junior, I'd been allowed to park my rust-bucket car here, to pick up the evening mail before driving it to the village postbox. During my first winter at Melusine, I'd discovered a blind spot in the security lights, and had amused myself by treading the tarmac to my decrepit banger without tripping them on. I used that knowledge now, stealing softly to the darkest corner of the Admin Block without awakening those snitching floodlights.

Now, for the first time, I could hear the muffled, rhythmic whirr of the injection-moulders rising from Old Factory further down the slope. They must be back to 24-7 production. This posed no danger, as night shift used only the small car park directly in front of Old Factory; anywhere else was strictly out of bounds. Nonetheless, a shiver rippled down my spine, as I looked up at the little white plastic-framed window, ajar by the merest crack, which had been the inspiration for my night-time escapade.

Maurice de Leny de Longueville, the factory's co-founder, had been a truly remarkable man. In May 1940, as France was falling, he had commanded a battle-tank in Colonel d'Armagnac's defiant counter-thrust at Montmaison. Captured, he had escaped; first, on foot to Vichy, then, as a stowaway from Marseilles to *Alger le Blanc*, where for weeks he had hidden in the outhouse of the café of a friendly *Grande Guerre* veteran, subsisting on dried dates and bottles of Orangette. Despairing of the colonies of West Africa ever declaring for the Free French, and inspired by his boyhood hero, Lawrence of Arabia, he had half-cajoled, half-bribed a camel-train to let him join them for the month-long trek south across the Sahara to Timbuctoo, disguised in Berber garb. More adventures had followed before he had reached the safety of Free French Equatorial Africa. Finally, he had taken and made good his sacred Oath, fighting his way back to France with General Martel through Tripolitania, Sicily, and Italy.

In the post-euphoric, exhausted aftermath of war, he had returned home to discover that his younger brother Maxime had succeeded in persuading their father, who had died in August 1943, to leave the tiny family château of Longueville entirely to Maxime, and, secretly, a large sum of money to Maurice, should he ever return. Probably, the settlement had been prudent and fair since, after three years as a Luftwaffe billet, and with their father in failing health, the château had been much neglected, and Maurice had been a known enemy of the Reich. Still, Maurice had set his heart on revitalising the vineyards. The dream had sustained him through the deserts of Africa and the brutal battles the length of Italy. His enthusiasm for the *Quatrième République* somewhat quenched (he'd shared his father's monarchist sympathies anyway), he had dismissed his chagrin with a pilgrimage of gratitude to Clouds Hill, the Dorset home of TE Lawrence, who had inspired him through the Saharan sands.

In the lounge bar of his seafront hotel in Bournemouth, the *chef d'escadron* had met and made the acquaintance of another wartime hero at a peacetime loose end: one Major Yaxley, late of the Royal Engineers. These two gentlemen-soldiers had been delighted to discover that they were old comrades, having fought side by side through Sicily and Italy, albeit armies apart. And they had shared an admiration for Lawrence, each carrying his *Seven Pillars of Wisdom* in his breast pocket. Within the week, they had become firm friends and had outlined, on a packet of *Disque Orange*, the essentials for an engineering business, which, sixty-five years later, had grown into Melusine. That early incarnation, Yaxley and Leny (Engineering) Limited, had been both inspirational and improvisational, turning its lathes and drills to any projects or products for which it had adequate manpower and materials.

I was confronting one of those early acts of improvisation now. The Administration Block, or 'Noah's Ark' as it was affectionately known, was a Yaxley-Leny self-build of the late 1940s. Bodged from whatever timbers and bricks the post-war bomb sites had offered – part Jack-built, part Jerry-built – over the decades the pitched roof of the long, slim building had subsided, leaving its gable-ends higher, like the prow and stern of a ship. The entry foyer was amidships, with the remains of the long-demolished first-floor bridge manifest in a stubby raised roof, reminiscent of Noah's deckhouse. The likeness was compounded by the whole nestling on the hilltop above Old Factory, like the Ark come to rest on Ararat, and by the occasional twig-bearing woodpigeon alighting dove-like on its apex.

The interior was no less eccentric. A bastion of creams, beiges, and browns, a corridor ran its entire length, with beguiling chocolate-coloured doors left and right, which, like the windows on an Advent calendar, kept secret whatever lay behind. After powdering her nose, the visiting sales rep might presume she was returning to the cluttered domain of her purchasing manager host, only to be confronted with the mops, buckets, gloves, and detergents stashed in the cleaners' cupboard. On his butterflies-in-stomach first day, the latest recruit to the factory floor might carefully count the sixth door to his left, not to find the personnel manager waiting with her prim induction manuals, but a coven of chatty sales ledger girls who would only disclose directions on pain of merciless, nosy interrogation. Any of us, after years or even decades at Melusine, might inadvertently gatecrash a bemused production scheduling meeting, instead of finding our own little dens and desks. Indeed, not a single day went by in Noah's Ark without someone blushing and blurting, "Sorry, wrong door!"

Behind those doors, the sequence of rooms was labyrinthine, with every room entered from the corridor in turn giving access to at least one other. Often this was a mere connecting door, but it might hide a stationery cupboard, or a kettle-and-microwave kitchen, or a grumpy, time-serving stock controller, or a mad-haired, lab-coated researcher, or the lost world of information technology, with computer pieces scattered across the grubby gold carpet like dinosaur bones in the Arizona desert.

Meanie de Leny kept a small suite of rooms to himself. From the corridor, you entered a luxurious lounge with leather sofas and veneered tables for relaxation and informal meetings. Behind that, lay the homage-to-the-eighties office where Faisal and Fatima had taken afternoon tea. Beyond that, hid the holy of holies, dubbed the 'executive washroom', home to an avocado basin, bidet and toilet, where, it was believed, Meanie indulged his best strategic thinking.

Now my eyes were fixed on the window of that celebrated executive washroom. That tiny washroom window, ajar by the merest crack. That tiny washroom window Richard de Leny was too mean to fix, blaming his own aversion to dumpy smells. That tiny washroom window through which I would steal…and steal.

4

Booty Call

Shit, I hadn't done anything like this since St Lucy's. I'd adored Miss Fagg's PE lessons. She'd hated me, but that hadn't mattered. Her imaginative, instructive fitness games and circuits training had been oases of pleasure amid the dreary tedium of the best-behaviour, plimsoll-toting classrooms. Our wet-weather favourite had been 'Pirates', where almost all the gym equipment and climbing frames would be rolled out to form an exciting, challenging Treasure Island course. The two chosen 'Pirates' would chase you, trying to tag you while you would dodge or leap or run or climb to try to keep out of their way. At no time were you allowed off the rough-and-tumble of mats, benches, horses, frames, or ropes. If your pumps so much as touched the wooden gym floor, or if you were tagged, you were 'captured', and banished to the Pirates' Dungeon in one corner. Often I'd been declared Queen Anne's Champion, as I'd climb out of reach to the very tops of the ropes where most girl Pirates wouldn't dare follow. But, oh, all this was over twenty years ago. Would I even be able to do it any more?

In the cold night air, doubts chilled me. Somehow, twenty lazy minutes every morning in my sleep-creased T-shirt and knickers, drowsily peddling my bottom-spreading exercise bike, scoffing my marmalade on toast and slurping my cappuccino didn't exactly seem the best preparation for my chosen career as cat burglar. I didn't even know if the window would open, or that the intruder alarm wouldn't go off. I closed my eyelids and inhaled deeply. Brace yourself, Fawley. Be ready to run like the very Devil.

I stretched up my black-clad paws, clawed the teasing window frame, and heaved it upwards. Good, open. Not a sound still, but the soothing whirring of the injection-moulders down below. Next for the really tough bit. The entire length of Noah's Ark, suspended from the overhanging eaves, ran a stout metal pipe which had once housed cabling for decorative external lighting. It now hid a hosepipe feeding the hanging baskets. How pretty it must have looked for the Coronation in 1953 with its factory-fashioned lamps, improvised from empty Orangette bottles, painted red, white and blue.

I leaped up, clutching the pipe with both hands, my tautening, tightening, aching arms seeming to stretch double their length as they suffered the agonising strain. A low "Woof!" drifted through the darkness, followed by the *ding* of the Gatehouse doorbell, telling me Pompey had towed Stuart within earshot. If I now made the slightest sound, or fell and hurt myself, I'd be fucked. Oh, please, Stuart…stay a while with Old Jim for a mug of hot sweet tea, and yarn about the new football season!

I clung still. Now for the move that had saved me from the Pirates' clutches time after time… First, I raised my little pump-clad feet to the window ledge, and the eternity of arm-racking agony ebbed. Next, I stealthily 'walked' up the wall, until my feet were level with the open window. Finally, I rested the backs of my ankles on the open window frame, and all I had left to do was wriggle through.

I smirked as I recalled this was pretty much the position I'd been in when Miss Fagg had detected my habit of keeping my knickers on under my gym briefs. Her whistle had blown, the game had stunned into silence, and Miss Fagg had shrilled, "Louise Fawley, you smelly girl! Climb down this instant!" To catcall cheering and jeering, I'd been banished to the showers at once, and 'Smelly Fawley' had been added to my catalogue of epithets ever after.

Now for the really tricky bit. Still clutching the pipe, I wriggled feet first through my cat flap, the hard plastic window frame digging deep into my soft calves. Ow, ow! My first mistake; I ought to have worn a pair of black skinny jeans. The backs of my knees gratefully grasped the window frame, and finally I dared ease hold of the pipe, pawing the overhanging eaves for counterbalance as I slid by the backs of my thighs into the blackness of the building. My rump stopped my slide and simultaneously my feet alighted softly on the wide windowsill concealing the cistern. Wriggling my bottom free of the frame, I bent my knees and arched my back to complete my ingress.

Oh, Louise, you clever cat! Mee-oww, mee-oww! Triumphantly I pawed and clawed the air, allowing myself a frantic feline dance, and *splosh*! – my toe stubbed something straight down the loo. I froze, fearful, ears enquiring intently of the inky stillness. Please, please, Pompey…you didn't hear that! I'll buy you a tasty, juicy bone if you didn't hear that! I listened. Nothing but the comforting whirr of perpetual production. Sinking and sighing in relief, I shut out that chilly night air.

Pouncing to the floor, crouching beside the bog, shining the soft light from my iPhone, I peered into the pan. A knitted Welsh-doll toilet roll holder lay hopelessly soggy, spoiled like a wet weekend in Aberystwyth, stopping up the lavatory, loo roll and all. What was it with him and seaside memorabilia?

Time to grab that mug and get the hell out. I crept through the half-open door into de Leny's office and, to my surprise, drank deep of nostalgia. The heady odours of Train Bleu Pour Homme, de Leny's favourite fragrance, formed the unmistakable top note, mingling with the middle note of lavender furniture polish, the ponderous bottom note of careworn carpet lingering longest. I closed my eyes and recalled the TV ad: the stylish sepia-brown couple of yesteryear kissing their au revoirs beside the Blue

Train, the cries of "*En voiture!*", the husky, dusky voiceover, "*Train Bleu. Pour homme.*"

Oh, sweet memories! At this very desk, de Leny himself had taught me bank reconciliations, had guided me through the labyrinth of extended trial balances, had educated me in the mechanics of management accounts, and had initiated me into the mysteries of analytical review and variance analysis. Latterly, we had collaborated on bank covenants, always engineering a quarterly pass. De Leny had been grooming me for finance director when my career had been cut short by my Big Win.

The well-remembered room slowly took shape through the gloom, like a ghostly grisaille. The familiar cabinets and chairs, the desk clutter amid mouse and keyboard, the madcap paperchase-in-progress of a modern, paperless office. The wall-mounted portraits of de Leny's father and grandfather, mere black tableaux through the greyness, thundered condemnation from their frames. "*J'accuse* Louise Fawley! *La voleuse!*" Every object seemed a silent witness to my trespass. I slumped shuddering into an armchair, palpitating, deeply breathing, desperate to collect my composure.

Had I reduced my own life to this? Was this the most I could manage with my millions, to steal a childhood keepsake from my kindly former employer, who had been more like a doting devoted father to me? Were it not for my Big Win, by now I'd have been finance director. Were it not for my Big Win, by now I'd have been engaged to James. Were it not for my Big Win… Oh, James…I'm still in love with you! Oh, James…I so want to have your babies! Oh, James…what has my money done to us!

Desperate, I seized my iPhone and my fingers flew frantically around the keypad:

> James, forgive me. I need you inside me tonight. I'm so at your mercy. Bring something to punish me with.
> Your humbled, contrite, ever-loving Louise. xxxxx.

Perfect. Guaranteed to bring him baying back, lolloping home like a lost Labrador. I wondered what would be in store. In a few hours he'd wake and get my text. Oh, James…

5

Soft Spot

I cuddled as close as I could to James in our snug, sweet-smelling mess of dreamy gold duvet and plump cream pillows. My hot, sore, self throbbed contentedly, delightedly. I ached for it again. Suddenly the duvet dissolved into shimmering, shifting sands, slipping slowly away, drowning the dreaming James. The pillows turned into pillars, the bleached bones of a ruined Roman temple. Maurice de Leny, clad in sweat-drenched desert-khaki, alongside a camouflaged jeep flying an oversized Tricolore, shrugged and gestured laconically as he said, "*Rien, mademoiselle, rien. Je suis désolé.*"

With a shocked start I awoke in the chilly greyness, my right hand still gripping my iPhone. My dulled, leaden head hung heavy, dazed. Oh, what time? Oh, how long? Holding my iPhone, gently I pressed 'Home', my spirits sinking to discover I'd slept through to 03:27. Fuck! Two hours, at least. I recalled my fevered text to James, feeling abashed and annoyed. Oh, what had I done? I'd capitulated, that's what! He'll know now that I want him! He'll let himself back into Kimberley and rule the roost. Doh, I'm a total twonk!

I wondered which malady was most maddening: to feel compelled to fight for a man you couldn't keep; to be stuck with a lovely man you couldn't love; or to love and loathe your man in equal measures. I'd had three serious boyfriends and had anguished under all three afflictions.

Giles (SBF 1) I'd loved with that totality of devotion that only first love knows, eclipsing every other source of happiness. Moonstruck, I'd imagined us together forever, through first mortgage, first baby, first school run. I'd disregarded those haggish soothsayers in Payroll who'd foreseen me dumped when the new-season office junior took to the catwalk. But when my replacement had been recruited, that fresh, fragrant lush-lipped Bitch had smiled, slinked and swayed her way into Giles' affections day by day, my defeat gaining a public and humiliating inevitability. I'd aped her style from her black bob to her pixie boots. I'd even mimicked her mannerisms and taken to tossing my head in her cute way. It had slowed the tide, but only because Giles had gloated on my squirming suffering, had adored my frantic fighting like a fool. I'd had to wait ten years for my vengeance, but ultimately, when Meanie de Leny had sought to trim cash outflows to appease the bank, in a true *Blue Peter* moment, I'd swiftly and smugly produced departmental accounts demonstrating that our head office sales team added no value to Melusine at all. Goodbye, Giles and Bitch. Revenge had been a dish best eaten cold after all.

Miles (SBF 2) had been the sweetest, supremely sensitive, most considerate and caring guy a girl could have wished for. If I'd had a big orange pumpkin and four white mice to boot, I couldn't have a waved my wand for a more magical lover. Intelligent too, it was he who had introduced me to coffee table books, or 'stuff books' as I'd nicknamed them, as in 'books about stuff'. Gradually, under his gentle tutorage, I'd supplemented the inadequate education slopped into my bowl at St Lucy's, strolling the path of self-enlightenment I'd followed to this day. He'd also been the handsomest boyfriend I'd ever had, in profile like a cameo of the Divine Augustus. But oh-too-good-and-gentle Miles just couldn't get me grooving. I'd found it an ambrosian delight to dump him. And Miles – oh! Miles had been so characteristically gentlemanlike about it, I'd almost wanted to change my mind and shag him silly and make him care, just so that I could dump him a second time and really, really hurt his heart.

James (SBF 3) had been the scruffiest, slobbiest sloth of the lot, but beneath those tangled ginger-brown curls his ice-blue eyes had fired love darts poisoned with lust-potion deep into my heart and soul. I'd panged and pined for him in spite of his faults and failings. I'd despised his rough, brogue tones, his ghastly grammar, and yet, one flicker of that scowling smile and I'd warm, tingle, madden, melt, dissolve. Oh, why had my malevolent fairy godmother betrayed my panting penitence and orgasmic obedience to that wild and wily wastrel?

The zip pocket of my running leggings was hidden high on my hips. There, aft, I stowed my iPhone before softly, silently slipping the telltale Chokka bar onto that cluttersome desk. Mechanically, unthinkingly, I grabbed that Holy Grail, that *Present from Bournemouth*, as if de Leny and I had been wrestling with a set of unmanageable management accounts which rebelliously refused to yield an operating profit from all five divisions, leaving us needing whip-cracking caffeine to kick us through the last gasp of our troublesome, toilsome afternoon, and deal us a royal flush of perfect performance.

My leaving Noah's Ark felt as unremarkable as leaving for an evening commute. Languidly, longing to be home, I quit that hallowed office as uncaringly, unsentimentally as if I'd be back for more later that morning. Slipping into the familiar-feeling washroom, clambering wearily onto the ledge-like windowsill, I edged open the larger, lower window. A rush of clammy, chilly night air mingled with the moaning injection-moulders. I half-looked, half-listened for sight or sound of Pompey or Stuart. What ideal luck – I observed the tracker torchlight flicker through the ash trees between the Marketing Block and the Tool Shop. In seconds they were safely out of sight and, swinging the window wide, I dropped down stealthily into the shiveringly cold, supremely starry, outside. The promise of another beautiful day beckoned, brimming with summer sunshine. Fuck James. I'd lunch and laze the day away with Helen in her beloved Hexhurst

Gardens, before spending the evening with my dreaded mother and staying there overnight. Even Mother had her uses, and a visit was obstinately overdue. James would find me genuinely 'not at home', that Victorian 'in a meeting'. You can keep your tousled tresses, James Doyle. Pah!

Firmly pressing the window shut behind me, I cut to the edge of the car park and, in seven triumphant strides, tunnelled that blind spot in the security lights to the seclusion of the pine trees. An ecstasy of victory electrified my veins. Yes! I'd done it! Oh, what a cunning cat! Mee-ow! Mee-ow! I'd known precisely where to park, the safest place to scale the fence, the tidiest line to take through the trees. I'd known Meanie de Leny wouldn't have had his window fixed. I'd known Stuart and Old Jim would've been yarning about football, not scouring for intruders. Oh, Miss Infallible! Mee-ow! Mee-ow!

I'd threaded through the pines to the perimeter paling. Clutching my *Present from Bournemouth* in my canines, I scaled steadily, stealthily up the mesh fence to freedom. Astride and atop, I browsed back through the gaps in the trees towards the slumbering factory in its sodium glow. How peaceful it seemed, with its murmuring injection-moulders easing out of earshot; somehow reminiscent of Bethlehem in Christmas cards, all flat roofs and somnolent, expectant, tranquillity.

I clambered down and felt free earth beneath my homesick feet. Smiling a contented sigh, I gratefully, gently closed my eyes, and promised to trespass no more.

Suddenly two strong hands grasped each of my arms.

My eyes sprang open and my mouth gaped wide in equal shock and panic. The mug slipped from my lips. A black-gloved hand flashed some sort of badge in front of my face. Every impulse urged me to scream, to shout, but petrified and immobilised, I mustered no cry. Then the black-gloved hand disappeared, I was forcibly pushed face first into the fence and my arms twisted painfully behind my back. I felt cold metal cuffs snap shut tight around my wrists. At last I managed tears, scalding blubbing tears, and a hardening, choking lump deep in my throat. No! Please not nabbed! No! Please it's a dream! No! Please not the police!

6

Down the Rabbit Hole

"This way, if you don't mind, miss, towards the off-roader."

The awkward twang of a young man from some part of London. With vice-like hands, one gripping the scruff of my fleece, the other clenching my cuffed wrists, he held me taut and hauled me leftwards. A brash black Voortrekker 4x4, all lumps, bumps, and tyres, dwarfed my dapper Mondiale 500. In the ember glow of the streetlamps, the chunky Voortrekker resembled some cartoon creature come to devour my cute Cinq Cent.

"If you'll please hold still, I'm just going to frisk you. It won't take a moment." The silky tones of a young woman, stepping into view. Thirtyish, prettyish, plumpish, and of

Indian heritage, at a guess. She wore a black padded jacket, black combat trousers and stylish black boots. She politely pawed my sides, then unzipped my credit cards and car keys from my fleece pockets.

"Well, let's not stand around all night in the cold." The plummy airs of a man, sixty-something, still handsome, debonair even, in charcoal-grey topcoat and slate-grey pinstriped trousers. He meandered along the grass verge, tossing the *Present from Bournemouth* from black-gloved hand to black-gloved hand, clearly pondering its significance.

"Open the back door, sis, there's a good'un," requested my captor.

Obligingly, sis swung wide the Voortrekker door, her big buttocks bulging in her combats.

"Bundle her in, bro," she pipped. "Let's quiz the naughty girl, find out what she's been up to."

"In, please, miss."

Resignedly, I clambered into the 4x4, awkwardly perching on the cold, soft leather seat. Bro released his grip from my neck, fumbled around my wrists, snapped shut my cuffs into some sort of restraining catch. I was truly trapped. Finally, he hauled my balaclava from my head, producing me, startled and stupefied, like a bemused bunny from a top hat, the ignorant, immobilised star of the show.

Bro shut the door behind me; *slam*! Sis slipped into the driver's seat; *slam*! Bro rounded the rear of the vehicle and into the passenger's seat; *slam*! Their black-gloved companion let himself into the back seat beside me; *slam*! With every slam I felt my impending fate. When I'd first joined

Yaxley and Leny, the engineering division had been very much alive and had long-held contracts to supply prison doors. Horrible, huge, solid steel things an inch thick. When I'd first been shown one, I'd suffered a panicking premonition that one day I'd end up serving a stretch behind one. Oh, please! This wasn't happening!

The black-gloved man placed the *Present from Bournemouth* between us on the back seat, as if he were advancing his king pawn. "Now, young lady," he began, "suppose you start by offering us your name."

"I shan't answer any questions," I protested. "Not until I've seen my lawyer."

"Now, you know perfectly well that in our profession, nobody is entitled to their solicitor. Supposing I begin? My name is Commander Charles Chumleigh, the young man who so charmingly escorted you to your carriage is Agent Daniel Smith and the young lady who so thoughtfully liberated you of your troublesome paraphernalia is Agent Charmian Mudher. Now, again, young lady, I do hope I've succeeded in making things a little easier for you. Whom do we have the pleasure of detaining?"

What was this? Who were they? I was suddenly scared, seriously scared. But what good would it do me to hold aloof? To know my name, they only had to browse my credit cards.

"Louise Fawley," I stuttered. "My name's Louise Fawley."

Mudher nodded to Chumleigh. Doubtless she'd inspected my driving licence already.

"And why on earth, Miss Fawley, have you been prowling in the dead of night around the grounds of Melusine Plastics?"

"Oh, please!" I sobbed and snivelled. "I'm so sorry! I've been so, so silly! I used to work here at Melusine Plastics. I thought it would be funny to steal that mug from my old boss!" I sighed and sniffed some more. "I saw him in *OMG!* magazine this afternoon, Richard de Leny, with Faisal and Fatima, drinking tea from this silly mug…and I thought, I thought… Oh, please! Please tell me I won't go to prison?"

Throughout childhood and adulthood alike, whenever I've been caught and cornered, I've always blurted my confession and contrition. I'd never been able to help myself. But pleading no defence had never moved Mother, except to a steely resolve to spare not and spoil not. In Miss Percival it had invariably cultivated a callous, caning contempt. I braved myself for another backfire now.

Instead, it was as if I'd offered to repatriate a long-looted Leonardo.

"So Richard de Leny is your former employer?" clarified Chumleigh, his voice acquiring an optimistic and opportunistic air. "Well, well, well!"

Smith started hacking hard at his laptop and Mudher fumbled frantically in the footwell.

"Sir," she ventured, "I have a copy of *OMG!*" Chumleigh shot her the foulest of glances. "I know, sir, I'm sorry, sir. It came on duty with me by mistake, sir. It won't happen again, sir. But I thought, in the circumstances…"

Mudher passed the publication to Chumleigh. There

was de Leny, his ginger goatee buried behind a gaudy Bournemouth, while Faisal and Fatima sipped china from the best boardroom Worcester.

"Well, well, well!" repeated Chumleigh, weighing the mug in the magazine against the one in his black-gloved hand. "So this picture inspired you to felony, Miss Fawley, and you might very well have got clean away with it too, it must be said!"

Might. I sat in sullen silence, humiliated. The handcuffs hurt. In my imagination, prison door after prison door swung shut in my face, condemning me to kaleidoscopic incarceration.

"Agent Smith, would you be so kind as to perform Green Due Diligence on Miss Fawley?"

"Certainly, sir. Miss Fawley, would you please confirm your full name?"

What else could I do?

"Louise Paula Fawley."

"And your date and place of birth, please?"

"The 25th of January 1979, in Bournemouth, Dorset."

"And your address, please?"

"Kimberley, Lepehurst Lane, Swansbury."

Smith – let's call him Daniel – tapped away avidly, assuredly. Any perceived awkwardness had fled from my fancy – he was handsome, hunky. A worthy successor to the wastrel James Doyle.

"And apart from the Mondiale 500, please confirm the other vehicles registered in your name?"

"Sure. I've got a Mondiale Maquis Sans-Chémin and—"

"Holy Cow! A Montvecchio Tarantella!"

"Mm-hm!" I sensed an upper hand creeping my way.

"The five-litre or the six-litre?"

"The six, of course."

"In Lethe Black or Diablo Red?"

"Diablo Red."

"Hello baby! Are you free later? This afternoon? Maybe we could hook up and burn some serious rubber together."

"Hmm…let me see…I don't have my diary with me just now but I seem to remember I'm pretty tied up today… oh, yes, that's it…I'm going to get arrested and spend the whole day in the cells."

"Agent Smith, I think we might all stand a better chance of getting home to our beds before dawn if you would kindly adhere to the proper line of questioning."

"Of course, sir. Just one more tack and we're done. Miss Fawley – ha, ha, ha! I wish I'd been there to see this! Miss Fawley, excluding motoring offences, have you any previous cautions or convictions?"

Even in the ambered darkness I must have coloured crimson.

"Oh, no! Oh, *please!* Not that! Do I *have* to answer?"

"I must insist."

Oh, whatever.

"I was cautioned for pulling a moony at a WPC in Lyndhurst on New Year's Eve, six years ago."

"Ha, ha, ha! She's Louise Fawley, all right, no doubt about it! Due Diligence completed, sir."

"Thank you, Agent Smith. Agent Mudher, what would

you imagine to be the going rate for mug theft? Seven to ten days?"

"Oh, at least. Could be twenty-one or twenty-eight days if Adelina Percival is on the bench. She always comes down severely on bad little rich girls like this one."

Miss Percival was a magistrate now? Could this get any worse?

"Miss Fawley," quizzed Chumleigh, "how keen are you to avoid prison?"

I winced at the inevitable 'P' word.

"Oh, *please*," I bleated, defeated. "I'd do *anything*."

"Then perhaps in exchange for resuming your freedom, you would kindly consent to performing a trivial task for us?"

7

Drink Me

"Miss Fawley," Chumleigh continued, "have you ever, perchance, heard of MI69?"

"MI69?"

"Please consider it absolutely no reflection upon yourself if you have not. There are cabinet ministers who are completely in the dark concerning MI69. We are, you see, minnows within the shoals of Her Majesty's secret services. I'm reliably informed that our annual budget gets lost amid the rounding, up in Whitehall. When it comes to power and prestige, you might say we're…"

"Sucking the toes of MI6?" suggested Smith, eyes glinting with mischief.

"Thank you, Daniel," retorted Mudher. "Trust you to lower the tone."

"Ours is not to track down the terrorist, but to sniff out the stinker, to ferret out the fraudster. We scavenge the scraps of no threat to national security, cases unworthy of MI5 or MI6, but which nonetheless require a little more lateral logic than plodding police work."

Surely some flighty, fanciful fairy had sprinkled her magic spells, leaving me deliriously delusional.

"We've had our eye on your friend de Leny for some months now," continued Chumleigh. "Cheltenham have been intercepting heavily coded messages to and from his contacts on the Continent. But after six months of surveillance we still don't have a damned clue what they all mean. We did think there might have been some connection with the Lakash contract, but so far as we can tell, that's all scrupulously on the level."

"We've hacked again and again onto the server at Melusine Plastics but can't find anything," lamented Mudher. "We've vetted everyone who's been employed there in a management capacity in the past three years, yourself included. We've even had people working on the factory floor and in the accounts department and as cleaners – nothing."

My head waltzed around and around like I'd concocted some noxious cocktail from neglected dregs of liqueurs and spirits and wines and had drunk too deeply.

"To be candid," confessed Chumleigh, "we came here tonight in desperation, hoping some spark of inspiration might ignite our imaginations if only we were to see this damned factory for ourselves. Nothing. At least not until you appeared, descending the fence with a mug in your mouth."

"What an inspiration that was…a real Brenda Broadbottom," pictured Smith.

"Daniel, you're so rude! Louise, we supposed that you must be a fellow professional," mused Mudher, "clad from top to toe in tight black. We wondered which organisation had beaten us to it."

"Though beaten us to what, Miss Fawley, we remain completely clueless."

"But I don't see how I can help," I whinged, "though I wish I could. I really don't want to go to prison."

"All we know for sure," confided Mudher, "is that the project is called La Ligne. Louise, does La Ligne hold any special significance that you can recall? A new patent or process, perhaps? It might have been just an idea when you were at Melusine. Please think. If only the commander can satisfy COBRA that Melusine has nothing to declare, we can all go back to chasing wine-smuggling expats."

"La Ligne? No, nothing like that when I was there. And I used to set up the cost codes for any new projects myself. Nobody could have posted a unit of time to anything new without my knowing."

"She's lying," teased Smith. "Should I tickle her?"

"But," I quickly added, trying to think my way out of trouble, "anything really secret de Leny used to keep locked away – *HARD COPY ONLY* he'd stamp it, and file it – he totally distrusts networks and servers."

"Quite the Luddite," considered Chumleigh. "Do you suppose he might have modernised his ways?"

"Well, his filing cabinets are all still in his office."

"And his key? I imagine he keeps it on his person and takes it home with him each night?"

"No, he hides it under a Cavalier Spaniel figurine with *Gift from The Black Country* on its base."

"Excellent! Well, Miss Fawley, doubtless you'll be delighted to discover how you might redeem your felonious self and avoid imprisonment."

I had been hoping that my inside intelligence might have been enough to loosen me from the strong arm of the law.

"We'd like you to take a quick snoop through those filing cabinets for anything relating to La Ligne."

"We've really no idea what to expect. You could be looking for almost anything."

"You can do it, Brenda. I'll stand at the bottom of the fence and watch you climb over safely."

"No. Absolutely not." I was adamant. "Nothing could induce me to set foot in that office ever again."

"Your final word?"

"My final word."

"Oh, well," concluded Chumleigh, resignedly. "We had to try. To the nearest police station, please, Miss Mudher."

"Very well, sir."

With a ghastly growl, the great Voortrekker engine grumbled from its slumbers. Mudher slipped the stick into first.

"Wait, no! Let me explain!" I panicked. "When I said nothing could induce me I meant, well, that I would never *want* to do it again, because it's felony and burglary and all that, but, I mean, if it's what *needs* to be done, for Queen and Country, well, *of course* I'll do it, gladly! Oh, *please?*"

"Stop the car, Miss Mudher."

The Voortrekker instantly soothed itself into sleep. I heaved a huge, slow sigh of relief.

"Miss Fawley, we shall be much obliged if you will kindly make a thorough search through those filing cabinets for anything connected to La Ligne. You might be looking for evidence of a business acquisition, of a new project or product, of some sort of smuggling scam, heaven knows, anything. Any papers you do succeed in discovering, we should be most grateful if you would kindly digitally photograph, with an electronic camera of my own nifty devising, which I shall demonstrate to you in a moment. Should you consent, I think I can promise you that later today the prime minister herself will learn of your glamorous gallantry. But should you decline, then, with the greatest regret, we shall be obliged to relinquish you into the delicate detention of the beaus and belles in blue who will, doubtless, ensure that you can expect your proper punishment."

"OK," I consented. "Give me the camera."

Smith slipped from his seat into the night, rounding the rear of the beastly big Voortrekker and opening the door by my side. Fumbling with the chafing cuffs, he loosened my wretched wrists. "I'll hang onto these," he whispered. "You might like to slip them on again for me sometime."

From nowhere, Chumleigh produced a tablet-like device, which leaped into life with a bleep.

"I must confess, Miss Fawley, that this is a gadget of which I am just a tiny bit proud. It's the only one I ever helped our old Department T design. Alas, with the demise of paper, it has seldom seen use in the field. It's quite easy to operate. You switch it on, here. You select your target paper size, A4 or A5, here. You activate illumination, here, and with this button, here, you take your picture."

"It's clever," admitted Smith. "It projects a soft glow, bright enough to capture a digital image, but more localised and less obtrusive than a sudden flash. And it looks just like a tablet."

"I understand." I nodded. I wouldn't have admitted if I hadn't.

At last, Chumleigh held out his black-gloved hand. "Good Luck, Miss Fawley. Truly, you are performing an invaluable service for your country." We shook hands. "Oh, and Miss Fawley, please return de Leny's mug – we don't want to leave any hint that there might have been intruders on his premises."

"I'll walk you as far as the fence, Louise," reassured Mudher.

We bundled ourselves out of the Voortrekker, me laden with tablet, mug and balaclava; Smith slamming shut the doors behind us.

"Chumleigh's a *sod* at times," bitched Mudher beneath her breath, once Smith was safely inside. "But," she conceded, softening, "he's a good boss and great fun to work for."

Mudher held both tablet and mug while I pulled my balaclava back over my head. Instantly I smelled James and felt comforted, caressed. Like a knight of old entering the joust, wearing his lady's favour.

"Good luck, Louise. Just do your best. And if you aren't back again in twenty minutes, I'll send Daniel to the rescue, never fear."

Now *there* was a mouth-watering thought. Perhaps I could contrive a calamity – feign a twisted ankle, mock an attack of vertigo. Hmm…

8

Once More unto the Breach

Alone in the thick of the night, again at the foot of the fence, I felt that same churned-up sick-to-my-stomach sensation I'd known knocking tremulously on the dreaded door to Miss Percival's office. Oh, please, *please*! I don't want to have to go through this again! I looked to my left to see the vicious Voortrekker standing sentry and, doubtless, behind its blackened windows, Agents Chumleigh, Mudher and Smith monitoring my meagre progress. Come on, Fawley, summon your steel – only custards crumble!

How I longed to unlock my Mondiale 500 and head home to my beloved Kimberley – to my steamy shower and my comfy, cosy bed. And when Jackpot James rang my bell later, he'd shag me senseless. I'd hug him, hold him, Dorothy-like. I'd learned my lesson. There's no place like home, and home is more than mortar; it's the people make the place. Home meant me and James and Gwynfor and Gloria and all my friends and family. Yes! I'd throw a party-popping champagne celebration for us all!

Well, clicking my heels together all night long wouldn't turn my pongy pumps into ruby slippers. There was only one way out and that was in. Firstly, fearfully, unzipping my fleece, I safely slipped Chumleigh's camera down the front of my leggings, quickly zipping up tight again against the chilly night. Second, sickened, I clasped that mug in my mouth, retching at the cold hard earthenware gripped in my teeth. Thirdly, tearfully, want-to-go-homefully, I started scaling the mesh fence again.

With my four paws, my gloves and my pumps, up and up I climbed. At the top I peered through the trees to the spectral skyline of low-lying factory rooftops, punctuated by untidy treetops, all rendered hellish by the ghoulish orange glow of sodium streetlamps.

Then warning *ding* and menacing woof as the gatehouse door opened once more, returning Stuart and Pompey to their nocturnal perambulations. That was a stroke of luck. It was well known that after his nightly yarn with Old Jim about the desperate scraps for footballing survival in League Two, Planet Stuart orbited in a different direction. His path would now lead him through the thicket of Nature Reserve, behind the brick-built Tool Shop, and past the pens of Polypropylene Silos. I had fifteen minutes clear at least.

Deftly descending, speedily sprinting, I arrived again at my casement cat flap. This time, after prising open the larger, lower window, I hauled myself upwards and inwards, arse and all, into the bathroom, its familiar avocado suite shining an iridescent green in the amber glow. Again I was in de Leny's lair. It was impossible to imagine him guilty of any intransigence. I felt certain I was wasting my time. But, if it kept me clear of the magistrates' court, I'd willingly entertain a little espionage.

Now, what had Commander Chumleigh made emphatic? Leave no trace of any intrusion. Carefully, calmly, I replaced the cherished *Present from Bournemouth* mug on its hallowed HMS *Victory* coaster, scooping and scoffing my calling card Chokka bar. Then, I attended to the drab grey-and-beige filing cabinets. Where was the Cavalier Spaniel? Charles, de Leny called him. There, his gaudy tawny ears discernible through the gloom. Silently, I swept up the tiny key, inserting it into the little lock. One dextrous turn and the ancient cabinets groaned open.

Now, would finding La Ligne be as easy as ABC? De Leny had always been anally alphanumeric. Surely eighteen months would scarcely have changed him. Creakily, squeakily, drawer 'K to N' rolled open. My eyes straining through greyness, I discerned my own girlish Carolingian script in thick black marker on the oversized divider tabs – de Leny had always been scarily short-sighted – *Land, Freehold… Land, Leasehold… Lighting, External… Lighting, Internal…*and…in a twirly, girly lettering, not my own… *Ligne, La…* Hah! Gotcha!

Greedily I seized the buff-brown folder, spreading its contents over the open drawer. Evidently, some sort of series of circuit diagrams or decision trees, on six or seven sheets. These would be a piece of piss to image, my maiden mission a certain cinch. Retrieving the tablet-camera from front of house, I remembered as best I could Chumleigh's instructions. I switch it on, here. I select A4, here. I shine the light, here. I snap the shot, here. Easy. Piss-easy. I rattled rapidly through the seven snaps.

Ugh, what was that reeky stink? De Leny really needed to Talc-o-Vac his carpets. A sickening sweet smell, like dog shit. The terrible truth dawned as I pulled at my pumps to inspect my soles. *Oh no*! The remains of a shitty splodge in the treads and…I shone the camera across the carpet… daubs of dirty doggy doo like diagrammatic dance steps in an old-fashioned *Teach Yourself to Tango* magazine. So much for nobody knowing I'd even been here. Sodding Pompey… first time I'd ever been snitched by shit!

As cat burglar I'd been caught and told to return my treasured prize to its proper place. As industrial spy I'd imprinted my mission in stinky, shitty footprints. I felt a frigging failure. The least I could achieve, despite doggy doo, was deliver these divulging diagrams into Chumleigh's curious custody.

One last look around the hallowed greyness of yesteryears and I fled, thankfully, clutching my camera, clambering up onto the water closet then windowsill, swinging wide the window, dropping down into ambered darkness and silent stillness—

"Woof! Woof! Woof! Woof!"

A clatter of claws and paws on tarmac, a salivating panting, a growling gaining ground…I nearly squealed and froze in fear… Fuck! I'd forgotten to peer out for Pompey! A warm wetness spread through my leggings as I frantically scrambled back through the window. I felt Pompey's nose nudge my behind before I sealed myself inside. From the orangey darkness his bark was petrifying, terrifying.

"Woof! Woof! Woof! Woof! Woof!"

"Pompey, ye wee feartie! There's nae anyone there!"

"Woof! Woof! Woof! Woof! Woof! Woof!"

Stuart must still be some steps away. I might yet avoid discovery. I slipped off the sill to crouch and cower beside the basin; Pompey insistently, impatiently laying siege with growl after angry growl.

"Hush now, my wee bairn. There's nae anyone there this time o'night. Hush now, my sweetheart."

Stuart was directly outside now. He first and foremost rooted for Rangers, Portsmouth an adopted love, with Pompey named to wind up the guys on the factory floor; most of them were Saints fans.

Stillness and silence. Stuart studiously flooding his flashlight intently and inquisitively into every cranny and corner of the window. As peacefully as I could, I unravelled myself flat onto the floor, my nostrils now nauseously close to a stinky splodge of doggy doo.

Stillness and silence. Suddenly my bottom vibrated. My iPhone! Oh, *please*, surely Stuart couldn't have heard! Secreted beneath my fleece, Mudher had missed my iPhone! But who was texting me in the dead of night? Darling James! Flushed with excitement at anticipated pleasures, lips parting in expectation of ecstasies, I hungrily retrieved my iPhone to devour his welcome, winning words.

Longingly I scrolled through my own text in panting reprise:

> Hames fourfive me. I neeed two inside me younit. I'm so at youe mercy. Being something to punch me width. You bumbled, contit, evil-living Louse. Zzzzz.

Hmm...not quite as I'd planned...shocking spelling! Now for my knight's reply:

> Louse, James has told me so much about you! He says he's sorry he couldn't text you back, but he was too busy inside ME at the time. OMG, he's GOOD! But of course you KNOW! You lose, rich bitch! Love and hugs. Miranda M. PS time I got some zzzzz.

NO! NO, NO, NO! Not mouthy Miranda Midgeworthy, most mounted of Sawhurst Stables? NO! Back in heatwave July I'd seen her, hosepipe in hand, splashing around the concrete stable yard, all wet white T-shirt and impossibly big boobs, half her arse hanging out of her skimpy denim shorts. NO! Not that slag!

The agonising apparition of my James entangled between her smooth but strong thighs and black riding boots made me thump and punch the floor in primal anguish, my heart hating and hurting. NO! Not that tart Miranda! How could he fall for such trash?

Then I sensed the bathroom window swinging open, and Stuart's searchlight beams start to pry inside.

9

Proposition

I clenched my eyes tight against the scalding wells of dread and defeat. I felt no wish to witness the intrusive beam which would betray me. To have been cornered making off with a mug, the world might have joked away as a jape, but to be caught clutching a camera containing images of some inestimable process or prototype…suddenly I was in serious shit. A better gamble by far to have thrown in my losing hand and risked a short stretch behind some purgatorial prison door for my foolish felony.

The unmistakable sound of shattering glass smashed the quiet of the night.

"Woof! Woof-woof-woof!"

"What the heck was that? Pompey, come back!"

Pompey was away, barking and snarling; Stuart's heavy steps yomping, stomping behind.

Surely this was my cue! Dear Daniel's decoy! Pausing to push my iPhone into my pocket, again I leapfrogged closet and cistern, then out through the wide window into the thrill of the night. I ran like I hadn't run in years, ran like it was Sports Day at St Lucy's, my housemates half-cheering, half-jeering me on to the victory ribbon. Directly across the black tarmac, bewitching the forgotten floodlights into glorious illumination, unslumbering the crows whose roosts lay in the pine-scented treetops.

"Caw-caw-caw! Caw-caw-caw! Caw-caw-caw!"

"Woof-woof-woof! Woof-woof-woof! Woof-woof-woof!"

"Caw-caw-caw! Caw-caw-caw! Caw-caw-caw!"

Pompey rounded the Marketing Suite and bounded towards me, a full hundred metres away. Daniel and Charmian willed me on from the safety of the mesh fence before me.

"Come on, Brenda! You can do it!"

"Catch!" I cried as I tossed the camera up and over the fence, throwing myself at the mesh in a frantic, feline grasping, all four paws clutching and clawing in anguished ascent. From the top I leaped to the ground, tumbling and stumbling, Charmian half-hauling, half-hurling me into the back of the 4x4. Pompey's rabid barks and Stuart's curdling expletives were drowned beneath the all-powerful, four-litre roar of the virile Voortrekker. Charmian sprawled on top of me in an impromptu girly scrum as the vehicle veered violently through one-eighty, then lurched into full-throttle, wheel-squeal getaway.

"Shit, that was close! Any luck, Louise?"

My lungs panting, my heart pounding, my throat gasping, I could hardly heave out my heavy words. "Ohh… ohh…oh, my…I thought I was caught for sure… Oh, my… That dog…that ruddy dog…tried to take a great big chomp out of my arse!"

"Relax, Louise. You made it. And we carry anti-tetanus. Daniel can give you a precautionary jab."

"Well, I've never heard it called that before! Hey… where is Daniel? And what about my car, my 500?"

"If only you would behave like ladies, ladies," chided Chumleigh from the steering wheel, "you might vouchsafe me the opportunity to inform you that Agent Smith has my instructions to deliver Miss Fawley's Cinq Cent safely to her home in the New Forest."

Daniel driving to Kimberley? Perhaps he would loiter for a nightcap. The possibility was delicious, invoking a tingling, thrilling sensation. Perhaps the climax of the night was still to come.

We untwisted ourselves and sat up, snapping shut our seat-straps as the Voortrekker hurtled onto the A31. Already the light traffic of dead of night was thickening with first-light-of-dawn vans and lorries.

"So, any luck finding La Ligne, Louise?"

"Child's play. All photographed." I smiled, smugly. "Some sort of flowchart, on seven sheets."

Eagerly, Charmian switched the tablet into light and

life, scrolling through my carefully captured images one by one. Her face fell.

"Oh, *Louise!* These are no use to us! You've photographed his family tree!"

Oh no! That couldn't be! I felt a heated flush of embarrassment and disappointment. "But…these were from the folder labelled La Ligne…I swear!"

"Jeepers, these must've taken him weeks and weeks! 'Reynaud de Leny de Longueville, Chevalier du Temple, 1256–1299'. Wow, you don't get this sort of stuff on runsinthegenes.com!"

"Oh, he's very proud of his family history," I pattered. "He's Richard de Leny de Longueville by rights. It's French. They go back forever…well, to the time of the Crusades anyway."

"Well, well, well! Please accept my congratulations, Miss Fawley. Undoubtedly, your discovery represents a tremendous advance for MI69. I have every confidence that de Leny's genealogies will prove to be, in fact, La Ligne…"

"As in *linéage*?"

"Exactly so. But the question is, why such secrecy? Why go to the trouble of encrypting what must be – if only one knows where to conduct one's research – publicly available information?"

"Perhaps the cypher they're using is somehow derived from the genealogy, sir?" suggested Charmian.

"Possibly. I shall take them up into Town with me later this morning. An old pal of mine does a turn at the College of Arms every Thursday. Let's see whether old Battler can make anything of them."

"Sir Nigel Naseby, sir?"

"Sir Nigel indeed. And now, Miss Fawley, it's time we told you about Project Godiva."

"Oh, *yes*, sir! Louise would be *perfect* for Project Godiva!"

"Hang on! If you two suppose I'm ready to ride through the streets on horseback with only my blonde bob to cover my boobs and buttocks, you can think again!"

"Miss Fawley, I might one day order you to imperil your life for Queen and Country, but I shall never expect you to abandon all decorum."

"Louise, Godiva is fun. Picture two businessmen chatting over their early-morning cappuccinos in a quiet coffee shop. They're our suspects. Another businessman slopes in, sits nearby, begins browsing his newspaper. Our suspects clam up. But imagine instead a waitress comes over, wipes some nearby tables. Our suspects carry on chatting. That's the essence of Godiva."

"I don't understand."

"Miss Fawley, Godiva is our flagship – though the concept is simple enough. We exploit the prejudices towards women's and men's respective roles in the workplace. For felons and fraudsters, traitors and terrorists alike, their awful, anachronistic attitudes become their Achilles' heel."

I was none the wiser.

"If the commander planted Daniel on a factory floor," began Charmian, "armed with a box of oily tools and a pair of greasy overalls, his fellow workers would trust him to overhaul Concorde. If he placed me in the canteen disguised behind an apron and a name badge, the same factory workers would just see a waitress."

"The point is, Miss Fawley," added Chumleigh, "which agent would be the most likely recipient of careless talk, the technician or the char?"

"Oh, I *see*. Male targets are far more likely to talk in front of a waitress, or a trolley dolly, or a chambermaid, because they presume that she won't understand, won't be interested, or can't possibly be anything more, anything other, than she appears to be?"

"Female targets too, Louise," resumed Charmian. "Back in the spring, I spent twelve weeks working as a waitress, trying to tease snippets out of two City Slickettes who'd meet most days in a well-known coffee shop. Both merchant bankers. For three months I lived the life – slumming in a bedsit, subsisting on my wages. Some days they wouldn't come in at all. Sometimes they'd come in on my day off. Some mornings they'd come in, and one of the other girls would get to them first. That was *so* frustrating. But eventually, my patience paid off. Just two words I overheard gave us the connection we needed – 'David' and 'Godmanchester'. That was all. But they slotted into the jigsaw perfectly. Now those bitches are each doing three years for fraud and embezzlement. Neither has the slightest clue who stung them."

"And a hugely appreciative City of London continues to be bejewelled by one of its most ancient and prestigious merchant banks."

"So…you want me to take a bar job at Lyndbury Golf and Country Club to eavesdrop on de Leny dipping his tongue into gin and tonic at the nineteenth?"

"*No*, Louise. He *knows* you!"

"Miss Fawley," began Chumleigh, "the encrypted communications traversing the English Channel are between Richard de Leny and his cousins, Léonard and Lionel de Leny. So far as we are aware, the two branches of the family have scarcely exchanged Christmas cards since the 1950s, until about eighteen months ago."

"Louise," added Mudher, "the de Lenys have a fabulous clifftop villa above Sainte-Modeste-les-Colombes, a gorgeous old seaside town on the French Riviera. We'd like you to holiday there for a fortnight – under an appropriate alias, of course – and soak up the place. Laze on the beach. Browse around the market stalls. Wallow in the tourist traps. But also, listen to conversations in the restaurants and the cafés, the streets and the shops. Observe everything and anything that might be significant. And above all, pay particular attention to any references to Léonard or Lionel de Leny, their families or staff."

Charmian whispered, "I wanted this mission for myself, lucky bitch. Don't you *dare* turn it down."

10

The Godfather

What need had I to ponder or pontificate? Was I one to hide behind my EuroScoop fortune and let other gallant guys and gals lay their lives on the line for me? Besides, surely Godiva would bring the excitement and adventure I had craved – and really, there couldn't be anything terribly dangerous in two weeks of sun and sea and…mmm… I licked my lips in expectation.

Evidently, while I'd enmeshed myself in genealogies and dog shit, Charmian had browsed her copy of *OMG!* There it lay, pressed open at the pictures of dulcet Duchess Charlotte and perambulating Prince Peter, which had delighted me yesterday afternoon. They seemed, Charlotte coaxingly and coyly, Peter cutely and charmingly, to command my devotion and duty. For Queen and Country then.

"Of course I'll do it!"

"Bravo, Miss Fawley! I felt sure you would relish the challenge!"

Charmian hugged me. "Welcome to MI69, Louise. Somehow I just *knew* you'd join us!"

"But, don't you have to vet me, screen me?"

"No, Louise. You were thoroughly investigated during our enquiries into Melusine Plastics."

"Besides," Chumleigh cut in, "I've absolutely no doubt that I can trust the daughter of the finest naval officer I ever knew."

This intelligence was like a leap from darkness into daylight.

"Commander Chumleigh! You – *knew* my *father*?"

"Did I know Captain John Fawley RN? My dear Louise Paula! At Dartmouth, he was my very best friend. And by the way, you're my god-daughter, don't you know?"

I could scarcely speak.

"You're…you're Uncle Charles…you're the Uncle Charles in my Christmas and birthday cards!"

"Indeed I am, although it seems an absolute age ago to me now. I last saw you at the funeral of my dear friend John, back in July 1992. You and little Adelaide in your chocolate-brown school uniforms."

My father's funeral had marked my final outing in my old Tickhurst Middle School uniform. I held the faintest, tearfullest recollections of the hot summer sunshine

In the pale chilly light of early morning, holidaymakers were stirring. In Billy Tugwell's tiny caravan-and-campsite, a big, bald, beer-belly man was waddling back to his tent, wet towel and flannel draped around his naked shoulders, his grinning, gleaming freshly shaven face gladdening at the sight of a skinny, curlered, dressing-gowned woman, with smouldering, sizzling frying pan in hand. On the periphery of Weldon's Wood, a brace of bulbous, Lycra-bottomed lovelies sat astride their mountain bikes, one poring over her mangled map, one preening her helmet-hair. On the closely cropped grass of Roundwell Common, the sturdy, thick-maned, ever-munching ponies in their gorgeous browns and beiges and creams, looked stoically from amid gorse and furze and pond as if to say, "These acres of England the Conqueror bequeathed us. Take them in peril of your soul! Dex Aie!"

Again those prim tones trilled from deep within the black plastic dashboard: "You have reached your destination. You have reached your destination."

Chumleigh, wearily, somewhat clumsily, swung the Voortrekker to a sudden stop before my white wooden gates, the tyres crackling onto the yellow sandstone chippings of my sinuous, snaking driveway. There was delightful Kimberley – its tiny tiles of red-ochre, its eccentric eaves of cream, its lead-latticed windows hid amid climbing deep-green leaves of camellia. Before my front door, all medieval with square studs of iron hammered into heavy old oak, my beloved black Mondiale 500 parked on a dapper diagonal.

"The vehicle gates open on number plate recognition,"

streaming through the round-arched colonnades of the parish church; of the long-gone wooden pews packed with well-wishers, family and friends; of six supremely smart naval officers carrying my father's coffin. Had I known the horrors of St Lucy's, I'd have flung my fearful arms around Uncle Charles' legs and begged him take me away. Instead, by the end of the summer, the tingling threat of St Lucy's had become the painful promise.

And that Uncle Charles had got Abigail's name wrong was sweetness itself.

"But Uncle Charles, why did you stop sending Christmas and birthday cards?"

"Hmm…you never received them, I suppose. Doubtless your mother saw to that. I often suspected as much. But a godfather has no real rights, do you see? And when I heard that your mother had sent you to a first-rate school like St Lucy's, naturally I was much less anxious for your future."

A first-rate school? More like a first-rate dump!

"Yes, an excellent school, I'm given to understand. My niece attended in the early eighties, before your time of course. Cassandra Chumleigh. She lectures in Classic nowadays up at Cambridge."

OK, OK, OK, so St Lucy's suited some. Anyone with brain the circumference of Jupiter or Saturn, and a cast-i arse. But, oh! My *witch* of a mother!

Suddenly the Voortrekker spoke with a voice lik lady on *Tiffin the Mule*: "At the next exit, take the slip At the next exit, take the slip road." Incredibly, alre were nearing journey's end.

I explained. "Please, please both come in. Gwynfor and Gloria won't be around and about at this time of the morning, but I'll soon sizzle up a fine full English and a pot of fresh hot coffee. Hey, I don't see Daniel?"

"Regrettably, my dear Louise, this time, we must all forego your welcoming hospitality. I mean to snatch some sleep before catching a mid-morning train up to Waterloo, then crossing Town to Queen Victoria Street. Charmian has two days' annual leave to use or lose before the end of August."

"Heading back to Solihull to spend a long weekend with my family. Mum is a Shakespeare nut. She's dragging us all along to see *As You Like It* at the Swan. Where *is* Daniel, sir?"

"Oh, he'll have sent Tiggi a text requesting a pick-up from here. Tiggi was our backup tonight, Louise."

Unmistakably, Charmian curled her lip on hearing the name Tiggi. But any secret significance would remain arcane for now. Suddenly swooning with well-worn weariness, longing for my fragrant, feather-soft bed, I inspired an infectious chorus of yawns.

"Louise, we're all delighted that you're joining MI69. If you'll only pop this postcode into your satellite navigational system," he instructed, scribbling with a pencil on a torn corner of plain buff envelope, "it will lead you to the lodge gates of our HQ, an old pile a few miles from Tewkesbury. When the porter asks your name, tell him you're Peeping Tom, and you're here to see Lady Godiva. Agent Trebarwith – Tiggi – will welcome you and lead you through your induction. Try to get there for about 18:00 hours."

This time, Charmian's face betrayed neither discomfort nor disquiet at the name Tiggi Trebarwith. Perhaps the two were love rivals for Daniel? If so, Charmian must be churning and curdling inside at the thought of Tiggi driving Daniel home. I was a bit miffed myself…

"And finally, my dear, dear Louise, above all, I'm overjoyed to be reunited with my god-daughter, the daughter of my old friend John, the very best of men. And, to be your godfather again, if you'll allow me. You can't imagine how often I've wondered how you've fared these twenty years and more."

"Oh, Uncle Charles, of course! You *must* come and visit me here as soon as you can! Oh, this is very heaven! And you, Charmian, too. You must *all* come!"

Clutching my house keys and credit cards, slipping sleepily from the Voortrekker, I slammed shut our waving au revoirs. Daubed with dog doo, damp-patched with pee, semi-somnolent I strode exhausted and exhilarated into the glorious, golden 'Good morning' of the rest of my days.

In meeting Uncle Charles I had reconnected with a part of me, the past of me. I felt again what it was to stride with my father side by side. The baritone of his manly, mannered voice, the spicy scents of his favoured aftershave, and above all, the strength and warmth and depth of his love.

Oh, how Prince Charming – Daniel had placed a tiny bunch of pink carnations on the bonnet of my baby Cinq Cent and on the tag, *Sleep tight, Brenda! xxx (car key through the letterbox!)* Clearly the flowers were petrol-station forecourt, but where else would a guy buy a bouquet on the A31 at five o'clock in the morning? Sweetened and softened by his hopeful, thoughtful gesture, smiling sleepily and slipping round the rear of slumbering Kimberley, I let myself into my very utilitarian utility porch.

I stopped and stripped beside my washing machine – balaclava, leggings, pumps and all, mingling in a smelly medley – sod it, I'd set it going after I'd slept. Naked, I trudged torpid through kitchen and hallway and up to my bedroom where, too tired to shower, I snuggled stinkily into my downy duvet.

Where was Plastic Friend? Oh, I've earned you tonight, pink playmate… Dammit! Doh, where was it? The injection-moulders whirred gently; Pompey woofed gruffly. Oh no… dog doo on the carpet!

"Rien, mademoiselle, rien."

"There's nae anyone there!"

"I've absolutely no doubt that I can trust the daughter of the finest naval officer I ever knew."

"Caw-caw-caw! Woof-woof-woof! Caw-caw-caw!"

Sleep tight, Brenda! xxx

Second Movement

Vetchley

1

Pit Stop

"Wakey, wakey, sleepyhead! Come on, cariad, time you were out of bed!"

Gloria's inimitable raucous caw penetrated my slumbers, bullying my wincing, sore eyes open to suffer the dream-defying daylight, her cartoonish face, all wire-wool curls and beetroot redness, peering inquisitively over my downy duvet grasped tightly between her ruddy gnarled fingers.

"Ooo is ee then? Seen im, I did. Sneakin out of ere at five o'clock in the mornin. Thought no one would see im, but Gloria seen im. Handsome bugger, mind. I said to myself, 'Ooh, our Louise has got a new fella! Not bad too!' Not before time, mind. Ooo is ee then?"

Oh, hell. The Welsh Inquisition. I so didn't need a dose of this. Instinctively, my hands fastened their precautionary grip on my duvet. "He's just a friend, Gloria," I ventured meekly.

"Just a friend, my eye. And is postcode scribbled on a corner of brown envelope, stuffed in your fleece pocket. That'll be to type into your Nat-Sav when you go visit im. Good thing your Auntie Gloria checks your pockets before she does your laundry. Looks after you your Auntie Gloria does, aye."

"You do, Gloria." I smiled, appreciatively.

"Well, let's be avin this duvet cover for the wash, then. Time you were up, my girl. Gone one o'clock in the afternoon, it is, mind."

Gone one? Chumleigh had instructed me to present myself at Godiva for six! I needed to shower, dress, pack... oh my! Gloria tugged obstinately at my duvet.

"Auntie Gloria!" I protested. "I'm...quite naked!"

"Just a friend, she says! An er lyin there in just er birthday suit! Oh, you're a sly one, Louise Fawley! A sly one, you are!"

"Auntie Gloria! I was too tired to go hunting for my pyjamas, that's all!"

"Hah! I bet you were! Lettin the truth slip now, she is!"

I was supposed to be a secret agent – I could scarcely confess as much to Gloria. Better she think Daniel a lover.

"Well, OK, I admit I am somewhat smitten. Daniel is his name. I only met him last night."

"I knew it! Romance in the air, sure it is! Gloria can

always tell! The flowers give it away, mind. Now, what you need to set you up for the rest of the day is a good hearty breakfast. What would you like, cariad? Your usual marmalade on toast, with a pot of strong black coffee?"

"Am I too late for a full English, please, Auntie Gloria?" I begged, in my cutest doe-eye tones.

"Hah! Full English! You've already had one full English inside you this morning, my girl, if I know anything about it! And plenty of beef in his sausage too, I'll bet! Hah!"

She relinquished my duvet, waddling and cackling her way out of my bedroom.

I'd acquired Gwynfor and Gloria with the Kimberley Estate. My then solicitor, a wastrel mate of James, his wits sozzled with scrumpy and drubbed dull by rugby scrums, had overlooked them, neatly red-taped amid the tedious legal detail of the Protection of Employment regulations. Oh, I'd been livid, figurine-flinging, saucepan-shying livid. James had fled to the shelter and safety of his rugby club bar. I'd armed myself with writs of redundancy and hefty cheques, before driving over to Kimberley Lodge to give them the old "you're fired".

But the moment Gloria had opened her front door I'd changed my mind. A wondrous warm welcoming wall of heaven-sent baking scents had overwhelmed me, with Gloria, all grey curls and red face and floury, flowery pinny, grinning gleefully. "Oh, you must be Louise! Come on in, my love! You're just in time for Welsh Cakes, fresh out of the oven, they are!" In I'd been ushered, into the tiny, tidy, prim and proper parlour, all floral wallpaper, dainty-lace chair-backs, gleaming horse-brasses and, all along the length of the sideboard, photographic mementoes of the black-and-white chapel-going long-dead, of flower-powered bell-bottomed children grown and flown, of grandchildren seldom seen, in cap-and-gown solemnity. I'd fallen in love with that sweet-as-cinnamon cheery old couple in an instant. Now, fifteen months on, it was painful to imagine Kimberley without them, without their delightful devotion.

I slid from my bed and stopped, stunned by the gloomy greyness lurking behind my creamy curtains. In England, we grin and bear so many miserable grey-cloud days that, when one dreamy dawn-tide the glorious golden summer sunshine brightens our bedrooms, it's always a delightful surprise. More shocking still is when, after two or three days, our English skies revert to their familiar grey. In forty-eight fleeting hours we convince ourselves that our weather always has been, always will be, Sicilian. What a deep and dire disappointment that first grey day inevitably and invariably is!

I showered until drenched in honey-and-aloe sweetness and serenity. Then, cuddling myself into my thickest whitest terry-towelling wrap, and bandaging my hair into a towering turban, I padded wet-foot down the stairs, beckoned by ravenous smells of sausages and bacon and beans. Gloria had prepared a feast: orange marmalade with granary bread, a pot of steaming hot coffee with crispy croissants, and of course, my favourite full English piled high. I scoffed my way through the lot; mouthfuls of sausage and croissant and marmalade and bacon and beans and coffee, all in a delicious, tastebud-titivating mush.

Gwynfor appeared at the patio doors with a child's pink plastic watering can, concentrating on the task in hand in his characteristically absent-minded manner, his pale bald round head rising from his silver-grey jumper like a chad from a dustbin. I rose and opened the doors to greet him.

"Yo! Lou-ise!"

"Hi, Gwynfor! How are you today? Oh, *Gwynfor*!"

As Gwynfor raised his right hand in space-traveller salutation, his left hand dropped, and with it the pink watering can, soaking his slippers. I pointed to his feet.

"O, damo," lamented Gwynfor, before redirecting the life-giving liquid onto the gaudy border. "Need a feed, they do. Not enough rain, see."

"Gwynfor, what are those called? The tall orange and yellow ones, like bottle brushes?"

"O, kniphofia, red-hot pokers. The colonel's favourite, they were. Reminded him of home, see."

"And the bright blue ones on the tall green stems?"

"O, agapanthus. The purple are agapanthus, too. Reminded him of home, see."

"And the bright orange ones with the big browny-purpley leaves?"

"O, canna. The colonel's favourite, sure they were. He loved his garden, the colonel."

"They make me think of bright orange handkerchiefs poking out of a magician's jacket sleeves."

Gwynfor wrestled with my feeble joke, his forehead furrowing, but it floored him. "All the colonel's favourites. Loved his garden, see. Over two years he's been dead, mind. Over two years already."

After his national service, Gwynfor had soldiered on with his regiment for a further five years, attaining the rank of corporal, before abandoning the Queen's Colours for a lifetime of odd-jobbing and bodging. Even at seventy-nine, he was happiest with a hammer in his hand; the rest of us were happiest when he'd put it down.

"Gwynfor, when you've finished watering, please will you pop the Tarantella down to Briers Garage and ask Kadir and Ilhan to valet it? It got pretty filthy the other day. I drove through an awful cloudburst on the A31, spray absolutely everywhere."

"Leave it with me, Louise, leave it with me," Gwynfor assured me, resuming his reminiscing and his watering.

I shut out the chilly cloudy rain-laden air, before padding back to my bedroom, where Gloria had cunningly arrayed Daniel's pink carnations amid sprigs of green in a lead-crystal vase on my dressing table, propping up Chumleigh's scrawled coded direction to Godiva HQ.

Quickly I stuffed a sartorial selection into a travel bag or three, but what to wear today? I pawed my wardrobe, wondering. Something high street, something Cohen & Jones– my beige suede bomber and my beige suede boots with a black polo neck and a pair of black leggings – perfect. When you clamber out of a Tarantella, nobody's eyes are on *you*.

I studied my mirror in a maudlin and melancholic mood. Wistfully, I wondered at my lined face, my drooping boobs, my paunchy tummy, my podgy thighs. Naked, exposed, each and every day of my thirty-something years was etched in my epiderm. A second time a shiver of self-doubt serpentined my spine. How could I go through with this? Louise Fawley…secret agent?

2

Whet My Appetite

From the safety and security of my camellia-clad old oak door, I snuffled at the chilly, grey day like some woodland creature nosing from her burrow, then emerged, clumsily lumbering my holdalls behind me, onto the sandstone-chipping driveway, where Gwynfor ambled in attendance on my Tarantella. Its luscious curvaceous Italian lines in ravishing famishing Diablo red were still filthy dirty.

"Yo, Lou-ise! She didn't need petrol, she didn't need petrol! I drove her down to Briers Garage like you told me, but she didn't need petrol!"

Oh, *Gwynfor!* I glared galled at my dust-encrusted bodywork and brakesoot-begrimed wheels.

"Thanks, Gwynfor. I could have sworn she was nearly empty. Open the boot, please, there's a dear."

Gwynfor fumbled with the key fob and, after arming and disarming the alarm several times, induced the little boot-lid to pop open. I crammed my bags inside, between the wide wheel arches.

"Gwynfor, I'll be away several nights, probably until after the bank holiday weekend."

Gwynfor looked bewildered, as if a weekend break was the last thing Sherlock might have deduced from my three travel bags. I hugged him, I couldn't help myself; my faithful retainer, in devoted dotage.

"Take care, Gwynfor. Take care of Gloria and Kimberley for me until I get back."

Gently I relinquished Gwynfor in exchange for my key fob and slipped through the driver's doorway into the caressing comfort of the supple seats of ebony leather. Seatbelt, *click*; mirror, yes – I looked perfectly purple-pouting gorgeous – ignition, OMG! My Montvecchio erupted into pyroclastic anger, stallions of horsepower coursing its chassis with the premonitory throbbing of an impending orgasm. With wild wheelspin my machine lurched into crackly-gravely getaway, as far as my electric gates, which swung in gentle obedience to release me once more into the wide, wild world.

I plugged my postcode assignation into my Sat Nav, the tiny Montvecchio icon plotting my progress on the navigation pane. Despite the piston-pulsating demons, my ride was sensuously smooth. With effortless ease, mile after mile disappeared beneath the wheels of that miraculously comfortable sports car. A31…M27…M3…A34…M4…M5…forest, factory, farmland, countryside, cityscape, church tower, all magically mingling into one kaleidoscopic trip to the tunes of Tchaikovsky, Mendelssohn, Wagner, Beethoven, Mozart, Elgar. It came as quite a surprise when Signor Sat Nav terminated my delicious drive with his mouth-watering, heart-throbbing, sexy, seductive Italian tones.

Robotically, I turned my Tarantella left, to face a pair of modest entrance lodges fashioned from a warm orangey-yellow sandstone, their guardians a pair of ludicrous layabout lions smiling stupidly from beneath their Restoration perms, all carved from the same soft sandstone, creatures as close to cute as any sculptor could muster. A tiny sign with gold lettering on an olive field heralded curtly: 'Vetchley Park Estates. Await attention'.

Creepily, a drab olive door in the right-hand entrance lodge squeaked open. Out shuffled an elderly porter in navy livery, a *Turf & Track Pink* secreted beneath his arm.

"Good afternoon, miss." His tone was perfunctory. "How can I help you?"

"I'm here to see Lady Godiva," I ventured, with equal helpings of excitement and trepidation.

"Whom should I tell Her Ladyship is calling, miss?"

"Please tell her it's Peeping Tom."

The porter sighed and smiled, his pale-grey lizard-like eyes enlarged by his thin-rimmed lunettes.

"Welcome to Vetchley Castle, Miss Fawley. I'm Todger.

Miss Trebarwith is expecting you. Please follow the road directly to the castle, then round to the right, and park in front of the fountain. Tiggi – Miss Trebarwith – will meet you there."

Todger pointed my way, with measured backward step, signalling my safe passage. My Tarantella suddenly felt nastily brash as it revved a bush-path between the languid, laconic lions.

Vetchley Castle appeared as drab and dismal, as uninviting and uninteresting a place as I could ever have envisaged. The castle, or at least the disproportioned façade I recognised from my stuff books as neo-Palladian, was hewn from a miserable grey stone, mottled with grey lichens. Its empty, expressionless windows echoed the slate-grey skies. An unkempt, uncontrolled line of deep-green leylandii blotted the land to its left. The fade-to-grey tarmac driveway, devoid of a single curve to break its monotonous inexorable straightness, was lined with tractor-hacked verges of rough grass, still strewn with massacred straw; only the flanking fields of pale-green beans enticed the eye at all.

As Todger had directed, I rounded to the right, between some miserable red-brick outhouses with corrugated-concrete roofs; one, semi-demolished, still sporting a line of old white porcelain urinals. There was the fountain, four ridiculous thick-lipped fish resting on their chins, supporting on their tails a badly cracked fountain bowl. I gently moored my Tarantella before it, alongside two Voortrekkers, one midnight blue, one midnight black; one undoubtedly my impromptu prison of yesternight.

Gratefully, I eased my aching self from my cockpit, and turned to confront the rear of Vetchley Castle. Greeting me was an unexpectedly welcoming, enchanting Elizabethan-Jacobean jumble of chimney stacks and gable-ends, of sparkling granite windowsills and dulled leaden drainpipes, of four storeys, four centuries of architectural anarchy. On the first floor, or was it the second floor, seven inserted, interloping, genteel Georgian windows, varying in shape and size from the large oblong palatial to the little oval lavatorial, appeared awkwardly anachronistic; on the rooftops, four satellite dishes wildly so. The stone, not so unremittingly grey as the frontal façade, was faded beige; along the ground, tubs of cascading orange – oh, what were they called – crocosmias, and bursting bright blue – oh, don't tell me – agapanthus, alone provided colour.

Oh, no! Oh, please! Oh, not now! Oh, this is so not fair!

Picture me out on the town – in Southampton, say – in the good old days before my Big Win. In the jostling push-and-shove of pub or club, surrounded by loud-lipped lovelies with big boobs and short skirts and long legs and high heels, amid all the drinking and laughing and smoking and bitching, one night in ninety-nine, one girly girl might inexplicably entice my eyes and set my heart rate haring. Oh, the ecstasy and agony of those mouth-watering moments, my wine whispering me on, my silly sense of shame reining me back. Oh, ever if I'd only dared! Instead, confused, I'd always clasp my secret safe.

But here, what chance did I have?

From a tiny door slipped Tiggi Trebarwith, attired in a lilac jacket-and-skirt with a purple blouse, her skirt breathtakingly brief and her legs lusciously long. About her cheeky-cutie face, her honey-auburn hair hung loose and long, her seductive smile sending me sizzling with every svelte stride.

"Hi, I'm Tiggi Trebarwith. Welcome to Vetchley Castle and to Godiva HQ."

"Louise Fawley," I choked.

"Oh, love you! You must be gasping for a snifter after such a long journey! And it's high time too. Where are my manners? Come on in. We'll fetch your luggage later." Tiggi slipped her slender arm through mine, then led me towards that tiny door.

"We're a bit thin on the ground tonight, I'm afraid. Once Rufus has given us dinner he'll cycle home, then it'll just be the two of us alone in this spooky old place – all night long. Oh, and old Todger down at the lodge, I suppose."

My mind dizzily delirious, I craved cool, cerebral conversation. "Why Vetchley *Castle*? It doesn't look much like a castle to me."

"Oh, it's a real old hotchpotch. The back – as you can see – is Elizabethan; the front is Restoration, with a later Georgian façade. The walled garden was built in Victorian times. The tumbledown outhouses you saw as you drove round the side belong to the Second World War."

"And the castle?"

"Nothing above ground. During the troubles between Stephen and Matilda, a henchman of Robert of Gloucester built a tower here. It's been Vetchley Castle ever since. After dinner I'll take you down into the cellar, and you'll see the ginormous basement blocks of de Tany's Tower, all blackened with age."

"Coo, those must be getting on for nearly nine hundred years old?"

"Last time Charmian and I went down we saw a big black rat. We stood and squealed and hugged until Daniel came to our rescue. Tonight there'll be nobody to rescue us, Louise. We'll just have to stand and squeal and hug."

As Tiggi stepped ahead to push open the door, I drooled at her proud pert heart-shaped arse, wrestling in its little lilac prison. Momentarily, a lead-latticed window revealed our reflections to each other. She had seen me; she knew that I'd seen that she'd seen me. She smiled secretly, triumphantly.

"Oh, Louise, I just know you and I are destined to become the best of friends. I just know it!"

3

Read All About It

"By the way, you've certainly served up a scoop for tonight's *Southampton Star*," intoned Tiggi, snatching an A4 sheet from the reception desk, and handing it, baton-like, to me. "Read this!"

> Pompey The Guard Dog Bites Your Bum
> by Sarah Scobie

> A cheeky cat burglar came away from her night-time heist with less booty than she started with after guard dog Alsatian, Pompey, at the well-known Horton firm of Melusine Plastics sank his fangs into her fleeing behind.

Night-watchman and former Royal Marine Stuart Finlay had nothing but praise for Pompey who, he said, had first laid a trap for any would-be thief with a well-positioned pile of poo.

"Aye, she trod right in Pompey's poo, and left a trail o' footprints straight to the MD's office. Ye've nae got me to thank, it's all down to Pompey."

Pompey disturbed the unlucky miscreant as she was delving for company secrets in the filing cabinets of Managing Director, Richard de Leny. Older *Star* readers will remember the manufacturer as Yaxley and Leny Engineering.

"This is a most perplexing attempted theft," said de Leny. "She appears to have been leafing through nothing of value."

The big-bottomed burglar apparently gained access through an unlocked loo window and de Leny added, "My former PA was always nagging me to have that window lock fixed. It's high time I heeded her advice."

The plump-rumped sneak thief was dressed in black from top to toe and had at least two accomplices, a man and a woman, who bluffed Stuart and Pompey with a perfectly timed diversion, allowing their hard-bitten partner in crime to escape.

Detective Sergeant Joanne Oates explained that hopes of early arrests had faded as the registration plates on the gang's getaway vehicle – a Voortrekker 4x4 – had proved to be false.

"But full marks to Pompey," she added. "He's welcome to join us as a Community Support Dog anytime!"

"Well, of all the bare-faced cheek!" I felt horribly hurt and humiliated. "Big-bottomed? Plump-rumped? I've a damned good mind to sue this Sarah Scobie!"

Tiggi smiled wryly. "Aren't you afraid that by taking her to court you might just blow your own cover?"

I clenched my eyes tight to blank my own stupidity. "Well, there is that, I suppose," I conceded begrudgingly.

"And don't you think it's strange that de Leny mentions you? Do you think he might suspect you? How many people knew that the lock to his lavatory window was broken?"

I scrunched my lips around and around. "Hmm, not many. I never thought of that. He's a wise old owl, de Leny. He might just have twigged."

"Well, fear not, my little D'Artagnan," teased Tiggi, "you're a Musketeer now!"

At last I surveyed my surroundings. The off-white ceiling was unusually low, with plasterwork orles of roses at haphazard intervals, rendered rough by century-on-century of paint-on-paint. The dark oak wood-panelled walls felt oppressive, as if any second they might start to grind inexorably inwards to crush us. A wall full of hapless country creatures – foxes, otters, weasels, stoats – peered from the panelling with dead heads. Beneath each, epitaphs evidenced their dreadful ends – 'Boxing Day 1897, 57 minutes', 'Ludwood Brook, 27th December 1899'. I shuddered, sickened by the senseless spectacle.

"Oh, we hate having them there too," empathised Tiggi, sensing my discomfort and disquiet, "the commander included. But they're part of our disguise against the locals. Vetchley Park Estate with its aged absentee landlord, tight as a gnat's bum, the castle crumbling, won't spend a shilling on it – still counts in shillings – but it's worked for us so far."

"But Tiggi, look at their little faces!"

"Take my advice and don't, or they'll be chasing you in their hunting pinks over the hills and hedges of your nightmares. Once, Charmian woke us in the middle of the night, screaming they had turfed her and were nibbling her alive. Perfectly horrid."

At that moment, two fox heads seemed to snap at me from the panelling, as a concealed door swung open, and a sly-seeming guy, lean and lupine, in chef's blue-and-white checks and three-day stubble, appeared, fag in mouth, and handed us each a cream-coloured card. To my heaved sigh of relief, I found him thankfully fanciable, in a not-a-lick-of-water-near-him, rough-and-ready, kind of way.

"Hiya, darling. Here, have a butcher's at tonight's menu."

"Rufus, this is Louise, our latest recruit. Louise and I shall be dining together in the Venetian Room."

"Hiya, Louise, sweetheart, pleased to meet you. Hey, Tiggi, she looks like she could do with fattening up, ha ha ha!"

"Rufus! Please don't tease! Just for being so beastly you can fetch Louise's luggage from her car and lug it all up to her bedroom!"

"Sure, Tiggi. I'll have a sneaky rummage through her lingerie while I'm at it, ha ha ha!"

From my jacket pocket, I contemptuously tossed my fob of keys straight into Rufus' snatch.

"Louise drives a Montvecchio Tarantella. It's parked by the Platypus Fountain."

"Hey, Montvecchio Tarantella! *Bellissima bambina*! Ha ha ha!"

And out he slouched, all lollop and legs and stubble and fag.

"He's a good guy really, ex-Royal N. All of the staff at Vetchley are ex-Royal N. Louise, let's skip that drinkie and make straight for dinner. We can enjoy a bottle with our meal. By the way, we tend to skip our starters here, but you'll find we're partial to puddings."

Thursday Evening Menu

Pork anise in spiced soy sauce with cabbage, carrot, granary bread; or

Fennel and salmon pie with puff crust, seasoned mashed potatoes, buttered carrots, cabbage

Eton Mess

Coffee and Shrewsbury biscuits

Suddenly my stomach seemed absolutely cavernous. "Fennel and salmon pie for me, please."

"I'm going to try his pork anise. Louise, which wine should we choose? It's the commander's cellar. I'm a total twit when it comes to wine. I just go by *appellation* on the label and I never go too far wrong."

"Well, you're one up on me. I run with the party packs of Schloss Adler. I have a box of red and a box of white on the go, pretty much all the time. The red doesn't last long when my housekeeper's busy."

Rufus returned from his errand, my three bags grasped in one hand, my bunch of keys in the other.

"Pop them up to the Green Lady Room, then we'd like dinner – one salmon pie and one pork anise. Oh, and a bottle of white and a bottle of red, please, but nothing too expensive this time or the commander will have Charmian kick my arse again. You know how she relishes *that* duty."

"The Green Lady Room? Louise, you *are* privileged. You've got Vetchley Castle's most celebrated ghost as your cabin mate. Ha ha ha! Keys!"

And with that he bungled through a hitherto hidden aperture, hinted by its antique brass handle, and, bags in hand, bundled up the steep staircase beyond, letting the panelling creak slowly closed behind him.

I cast an angry glance at Tiggi. "*Ghost?*"

"Oh, please don't tell me you believe in ghosts and ghoulies? The Ghost of Lady Arabella Maleffant…whooooo! They say she summered here in 1645, after eloping with her lover, a captain in the King's infantry. When a trooper arrived to tell of the King's defeat at Naseby, and the death of her lover in the thick of battle, she fled upstairs and threw herself from the rooftop. They say you'll see her spirit, with auburn hair and emerald dress, embroidering in the window seat. Then you'll hear the ghostly hooves of the trooper's horse outside and see her rise with fearful face to learn her lover's fate…"

"Oh, *don't!* Or I'll be too scared to sleep alone in there! I'll—"

"Whooooo! Go on, freshen up. I've got some paperwork to file away, and Rufus will be at least half an hour. Your room is dead ahead of you at the top of the stairs. I'll knock for you at about eight?"

"Eight sounds absolutely fine."

And my arms held fast by Trepidation and Resignation, those callous gaolers escorted me through the still-not-shut panelling, and up the dingy ill-lit staircase, all chocolate-brown paint and liquorice-black linoleum, to await my fate in the Green Lady Room.

4

Tiggi's Tale

I clambered the dingy dark staircase, pushing open the unpromising chocolate-brown door, to discover that the Green Lady Room was absolutely charming. The classic calm of its delicious décor was softly soothing. Sweet vanilla ceiling, scrumptious custard walls, freshly baked gingerbread carpet – home-cooked heaven to a hungry girl. With childish delight and gleeful yippee, I leaped longingly onto my lemon meringue bed and purred like a happy cat. My secret agent adventure had truly begun.

Belatedly, evening sunshine dispelled the miserable greyness of the day, invoking a golden glow from the burnished curtains. Dragging myself from my super-soft pie, I cracked open a can of cola from the bedside bar, and stood, sipping, staring at the Vetchley vista, serenely steeped in sunlight.

Below, the brace of beastly, clumsy Voortrekkers bullied my tiny, lithe Tarantella. It felt as if I had known Vetchley Castle all my life. Had I *really* arrived for the first time only twenty minutes ago?

A door downstairs slammed, the bedroom window rattled, and crossing the car park, Tiggi appeared, bulging black bin sack in hand. My first flushes of flustered fancy had faded, yet, I thrilled anew at her sweet-and-sexy sway, her butterscotch brown slender legs, her auburn mane caressing her neck and lapping her back. Oh, *what*! No female form had ever so dizzied and disoriented me before. What did it *mean*?

My iPhone held three texts: one from Mother, insisting I lunch with my scowling sister and nasty niece on Bank Holiday Monday; one from Gloria, reminding me to pop a pack of condoms in my pocket; and one from Jade, mortified for missing me, grovelling for getting her diary awry, offering the olive branch of a free treatment. Oh, my grotty, snotty green nail polish – what would *Tiggi* think?

The central heating clattered and clanged into life. Already sweltering in jacket and jeans, I'd need to change or I'd bake like Hotchi the Hedgehog. In my last few moments of shove-it-in-anyway packing, I'd stowed an ancient favourite into my pink holdall, a little black dress that had cost me a fiver five years ago at Factory Favourites. I'd celebrated in that dress, bouncing skunk-drunk to boy bands at cheeralong concerts. I'd copulated in that dress, bare arse on the grass, thighs wide and welcoming. I'd pissed on that dress, squatting, sharing a seat in the ladies' loo of a ram-packed pub. I'd puked on that dress, on my semi-somnolent, staggering, sickening, serpentine struggle home. That little black dress was a survivor, stained with impregnable memories, sullied with cheerfulness and confidence. Whatever fun I flung at my little black dress, time after time it scrubbed up like a genuine Gianetta. Whatever trouble Tiggi might throw at it tonight, together my little black dress and I would trounce it.

Knock-knock-knock.

"Are you ready, Louise?"

I opened my door to greet my tantalising temptress. "Of *course*!"

"Oh, I *adore* your dress! It so suits you!"

"What, *this* old thing? As they say in the movies! I only packed it because it travels well."

"You're positively glittering. Allow me to escort you to dinner. The Venetian Room is just next door."

I'm positively gushing, I thought. Tiggi had ditched her little lilac jacket. Her bountiful boobs proffered themselves like forbidden fruit in the clasp of a sweetly smiling grass-skirted maiden. Her purple shirt pinched at her tiny tight waist, accentuating her wildly writhing behind as she strode ahead.

"This is the Venetian Room. We're all rather proud of it. It's something of a team effort. Come on in."

My greedy gaze fixed inexorably on the inimitable carnival of colour, the unmistakable pageant of sky and sea, of an original Antonio Canal, where a pair of golden gondolas, glistening resplendent, drifted gaily amid a swarm of smaller sculls, before a sun-soaked *Palazzo Ducale.*

"I can see that you know your art. The Canaletto was a gift of gratitude from Baybutts Bank last year. Charmian enjoyed a spot of luck and pinned a couple of rogue traders. The bitches had been costing the bank billions. Then it was Daniel's idea to rejuvenate what had been a dump of a room along a Venetian theme, make a sort of common room out of it. The commander donated the glassware. It's modern, but rather good, don't you think? He picked it up on some mission or other to an island in the lagoon, oh, years ago. Daniel cut and hung the Venetian-Gothic window coving. He *is* canny with his carpentry."

"Oh, it *is* a lovely room!"

"I found all the watercolour prints on bid-monkey. com. The extent of my contribution, I'm afraid."

Rufus crashed through the door, fag in hand, careering a Hot Hostess trolley.

"Hi, girls! One salmon pie, one pork anise, for your kind delectation. Your Eton Mess is in the fridge, with two bottles of white, one dry and one sweet. Oh, and two bottles of claret on the sideboard."

"Rufus, thank you," said Tiggi, beaming.

"You pair don't mind playing waitresses, do you? Only Lisa is doing her nut. Our youngest, Nathan, started teething today and he's howling one hell of a hullabaloo."

"Of course not. You go. Poor little Nathan. Give my love to Lisa."

"Cheers, Tiggi. 'Waitresses' will be a cool kinky dressing-up game for you both anyhow, ha ha ha!"

And he was gone again, like a rat scurrying back down a drain.

"Oh well," said Tiggi with a resigned sigh, "Waitresses it is. Louise, you pour the dry white, I'll lay our dinners out."

The bottle was beautifully chilled, and thoughtfully uncorked. The golden elixir flowed into the crystal goblets with a delicious *tonk-tonk-tonk*, its heavenly nosegay mingling with fragrances of fennel and salmon, aromas of aniseed and pork, and scents of seasonal vegetables.

"Bottoms up!" I cheered.

"Oh, *don't*," groaned Tiggi. "Our headmistress used to say that before she spanked us. She found it funny too, sadistic bitch!"

"No need to go *there*. School was a painful process for me too," I rued. "What did you venture into after your schooldays? Did you always have a hankering for the old cloak-and-dagger?"

"Of course not!" chuckled Tiggi, then, inexplicably, her chestnut eyes grew and glistened, her lower lip quivered, and telltale tears crept onto each of her cheeks.

"*Tiggi*! What *is* it?"

"Better out than in, I guess." Tiggi stifled and sighed, damming back the salt-tide with blink after blink.

"I grew up on the family farm in Cornwall. On the North Coast, a few miles south of Tintagel. You might imagine it idyllic, until you realise that farming was well and truly becalmed in those days. Even the weevils in the cowpats fell under fixed and floating charges to the blasted bank. Mum and Dad worked like stink to hold their four farms together – my elder brother Piran mucking in too – but once in a while when the weather was at its brightest and best, they'd treat themselves to their one indulgence – sailing.

"I'd just graduated – in History – and was squandering my summer days skulking around, wondering what to do with the whole of the rest of my life. One glorious afternoon – sunny and breezy, perfect for sailing – Mum and Dad set out for a few precious hours in their yacht, the *Petroc*. They were completely and contentedly at home on the wild waves around their beloved Cornish coast. But they never came home. By evening, Piran was pacing the kitchen, wondering whether we should call the coastguard, or go milk the cows without Mum and Dad, when two police cars came trundling down our farm track. Instantly we knew, we both just knew. And we knew that we'd known all along.

"The *Petroc* had blown onto Deadman Rocks and smashed into splinters. Next day, a family on holiday heard the news and contacted the police to inform them that when they'd been picnicking on the clifftops the afternoon before they'd seen a yacht sailing straight for shore, but not knowing the coast they had supposed that a cove lay below and out of sight. The news made absolutely no sense. Mum and Dad were both experienced sailors. It was as if they'd deliberately dashed themselves to their deaths.

"It took almost fifteen months to unravel our parents' financial affairs. The life insurance companies howled like the hounds of hell but had to pay up in the end. Piran took the two best farms and the farmhouse. I took the other two and rented them back to him, with the studio cottage to live in.

"Then, one dreadful howling wet November night, there was a rat-a-tat-tat at my door. I imagined it was Piran, but instead it was a stranger, doing his best in the wind and the rain with a black umbrella, dreadfully drenched in his charcoal topcoat. 'Miss Tiggi Trebarwith?' he'd asked, and before I could reply, had added, 'My name is Commander Charles Chumleigh. My organisation holds incontrovertible evidence that your parents were murdered by a gang of drug smugglers with whom they were unlucky enough to cross tack as the brigands unloaded their cargo. Might we count on your co-operation in their capture this very night?' And that, Louise, was how the commander recruited me to MI69."

5

First Fall

Throughout Tiggi's discourse, transfixed by her tale, my mind enmired in imaginings of geese and ducks frantically farmyard-flapping amid tumbledown outbuildings; in visions of a taut-lipped twenty-something Tiggi, Demelza-like, defying the lightning to strike her; in images of a bright white yacht cutting through sun-sparkling surf on its death-trajectory towards those ragged rocks. I had pierced a parallel Cornwall to that described in the Venetian Room; my re-entry into reality was bewildering. Any touches or traces of heartache or hurt had fled Tiggi's face; I saw only stony strength.

My gosh! Weather away her languid luscious-in-lilac

look, beneath she's as granite-tough as a Cornish tor. And I'm panting and panging for this princess? Heaven help me!

Tiggi turned to more hearty hankerings. "Louise, our dinners! They'll be stone cold! Let's sit and eat."

The long, lean, brown-oak dining table, dripping with cream Venetian lace, divided the common chamber between utilitarian entry-end with silver refrigerator and grey-pine sideboard, and comfy, cosy, window-end, with two three-seater settees upholstered with gay, gaudy gondoliers ferrying pert, pouting pretties, before the easy, effortless weight of the Ponte Rialto. Tiggi sat with her back to the window, the gathering gloaming enveloping the long, low escarpment outside, lending her expression a demonic darkness. Awestruck, I wondered whether the Tiggi of Sunshine or the Tiggi of Darkness had snapped shut my shackles, had fired that fatal lust-bolt into my shocked, sizzling self.

"So," I stuttered, mustering every effort to compose and control my bronco-bucking urges, "did you help Uncle Charles capture the drug gang? I'll bet he had you out in that wet and windy weather!"

I'd hoped that playing the 'Uncle Charles' card might have halted Tiggi's hand. Instead, she took another trick with demure demur.

"Not at all," tittered Tiggi. "My bungalow sits at the head of jagged Polgarreg Cove, and boasts the only pathway down to the shingle beach – such as it is – for nearly two miles. The commander requisitioned my kitchen as his

Forward HQ, that's all – with me and my espresso machine, of course."

"Then, whatever had happened to your parents?"

"One of the gang, Josh, was a local man. It was his idea to land their poisonous load at low tide on the slender beach, way below the cliffs and out of sight, then smuggle the drugs up and inland long after dark. Polgarreg is a forgotten spot, only known to us locals. But when the *Petroc* unexpectedly crossed their tack, the gang got jumpy. They hauled themselves alongside her and boarded."

"Oh my gosh – your poor parents!"

"Josh knew my father, had odd-jobbed for him. He watched helpless and horrified as my father and mother in turn were struck on the backs of their heads and bundled unconscious into their cabin. Then the *Petroc* was rigged cunningly, cruelly, to send her sailing straight for shore, right onto the rocks…"

Tiggi's voice faded, faltered. Her face whitened, her eyes widened; at length, she visibly winced.

"Then, nearly twelve months later, Josh plucked up the courage to turn Queen's Evidence. He…"

Now Tiggi blubbed and blurted hot salt tears. Instinctively, unthinkingly, I rose and flung my arms around her shoulders, our heads nuzzling, blonde and auburn mingling.

"Louise," she sobbed, with a sniff. "I'm OK. Really, I'm OK. I'm better if I don't think about it, don't talk about it."

She unclasped my arms from her neck and held my wrists tight, our faces so close I felt her sweet zephyr breath caress my cheeks. The tips of our noses touched. Her beautiful, bountiful big brown eyes seemed as quicksand, dragging me down, dragging me in. My lips gently parted, gently puckered.

"Louise, our meals! And after all Rufus' hard graft! Sit! And tell me what it's like to win EuroScoop!"

I did more than that. I unfolded, napkin-like, my entire life story, from that happy childhood land where Daddy John and Uncle Charles had been my playmates, my protectors, to my father's dreadful death, heralding the intolerable horrors of St Lucy's, and Miss Percival's inescapable cane; to my first frantic romance with Giles; then miserable wet Sunday afternoon upon miserable wet Sunday afternoon leafing lazily through stuff books while Miles catalogued and re-catalogued his weird CD collection; to my final angry acrimonious altercation with James, six whisky-tumblers shied at his coconut head.

The delighting dry white lubricated our lips as we gossiped and gorged, me scoffing my salmon pie between mouthfuls of conversation, Tiggi picking at her pork anise as she listened, with inquisitive eyes. Our disarming dessert wine let loose laughter, as we stuffed our sweet and sticky Eton Mess, and at last, amid mints and shortbread, the caressing claret soothed and softened us into a sensuous sorority.

"*Men!*" moaned Tiggi, glowering. "I've *completely* given up on them. I mean, they're so *predictable!*"

"Oh, you're so *right*," I concurred. "I make the merest mention of my Montvecchio Tarantella and I get 'Hey, *bellissima bambina!*' Without fail. As if any true Italian Stallion would wolf-whistle 'Hey, *bellissima bambina!*' at a glimpse of a girl with a sports car!"

"I'll gazunder that. My last boyfriend, he'd be snuggled sweetly between my thighs, primed to please, guaranteed he'd holler, 'Crouch! Touch! Pause! Engage!' Oh, ha bloody rugby ha."

A snigger leaped loose from my lips.

"Oh, *Louise*! You're every bit as bad as they are! You're…"

"Oh, *Tiggi*! I'm not! Really I'm not! I *promise* I'm not! I'm…um…how was your pork anise?"

"Disappointing. Not what I'd expected at all. But then, I'm a passionate believer in seeking fresh experiences. I always make myself try new things, even when I'm certain I won't enjoy them. Then normally I'm pleasantly surprised. Do *you* savour the plunge, Louise? Do *you* relish experimenting?"

"I – I – my Grand Tour of Europe was pretty spontaneous, I suppose."

"That's when we first became interested in you. MI69, I mean."

"I don't understand."

"We largely disregarded all ex-employees when we trawled through the Melusine personnel files. It seemed sensible that anyone tangled up in La Ligne would still be on board ship. Then *you* cleared off to the Continent. It seemed suggestive."

"Barking up the wrong dog, I'm afraid."

"We'd concluded so. But then last night when we pinned your signal to Melusine Plastics premises…"

"Pinned my signal?"

"Oh, shit. I shouldn't have said that. Damn this Château Diable."

With aghast and awestruck horror I beheld the truth. "My phone! My iPhone! You've tracked me on my iPhone! My texts! My emails! Oh!"

"Chumleigh's going to *fry* me! Oh, please don't say I've told!"

"*I'm* going to fry you! I'll—"

"Tell Sarah Scobie of the *Southampton Star*, 'Hey, I'm the plump-rumped sneak thief. I want to make a full confession to your readers, and guess what, there's a secret service unit called MI69 who've been sat-tracking my iPhone'?"

"Oh, *Tiggi*! How *could* you? You caught all my calls?"

"Mm-hm!"

"You read all my texts?"

"Mm-hm!"

"You've seen all my emails?"

"Mm-hm!"

"Oh, whatever must you *think* of me?" I squirmed at the shameful, painful recollection of my bitch-and-snitch phone calls, my flirt-and-dirt messages, my tease-and-sleaze emails.

Tiggi whispered calmly, candidly. "Actually, I like you lots. I really, really like you, Louise."

From the pipes of the central heating arose a nauseating whining, then sudden, sullen silence.

"Damn, it's gone off. Louise, let's move down onto the

sofas. It stays cosier for longer up that end."

We did so, Tiggi steadying herself on the final bottle of claret, decanting the rich liquid into a browny-burgundy glass goblet, studded with gold-set garnets, placed with pride on a tiny occasional table.

"I bet *you*…" Tiggi slipped and slurred her words, "I bet *you* – you can't take your knickers off without lifting your bum from your…sofa. Take your…ker-nickers off, and pop them on the…little table."

"Oh, that's easy!" I bragged and blustered. "Easy-peasy. Peasy-easy. But *you* first, Tiggi-Wiggi!"

"Gladly, but remember the loser has to gown the doblet in one!"

Tiggi slipped her hands up either side of her skirt, wriggling and writhing from butt cheek to butt cheek, tugging this way then that way at her stubborn shorts. Then, that triumphant smile spread and shone wide as she hauled her pretty lilac panties down around her beautiful butternut thighs. She allowed them to fall around her ankles, then fished them from the floor with clenched toes, dropping them daintily next to the goblet. Doh! Lilac nail polish! Trust that girl to be completely colour-co-ordinated!

"*Your* turn, Louisey, easy-peasy!"

Confidently, I slid my palms up the sides of my thighs, under my little black dress, right to my bulging buttocks but – I couldn't reach to grab at my thong! NO! There *had* to be another way! Desperately, I buried both hands deep between my thighs, grasped my gusset and hauled and hauled – and with tug after tug felt my thong ride tighter, higher, tauter.

"I *can't!*" I whinged, dreading defeat.

"Ha! Ha! Easy-peasy, yeah? Peasy-easy, huh? Open your throat, Louisey-Peasy!"

I tugged remorselessly, remorsefully, at that cheating, chafing thong, while Tiggi grasped the gaudy goblet and presided, priestess-like, to administer her enslaving elixir.

"Oh, I *can't!*" I wailed like a spoiled child. "It won't budge! I'm well and truly wedgied!"

"Then drink. You lose. You know it makes sense to surrender."

Tiggi tipped the brimming brown bowl to my mouth, its delicious but infectious, sweet yet sickening wine washing my tingling tongue, splashing my tickling chin. I giggled, I gurgled, I coughed, I choked. I fell flat onto my back, Tiggi tumbling atop. In expectation of exquisite ecstasies and pulsating pleasures, I clenched my eyes tight, gaping, gasping.

"Kiss me, Tiggi!" I whispered. "Kiss me, *please*! Kiss me, I *beg* you!"

A sudden shudder snaked my shoulders, as if ghosts of ages past had seeped from the old stones to tease and taunt me – the victims of Vetchley of yesteryear – the ravished, the ridiculed, the robbed, the strangled, the smothered, the starved – all mocked my drunken seduction.

Our puckered mouths gelled in an exquisite, ecstatic, longing, lingering kiss. Then Tiggi lifted her lips from mine. I resumed my gasping and gaping, unclenching my eyes to witness her strangely stern face.

"Come on. It's time we went to our beds. The

commander will be here by seven o'clock in the morning, and he'll expect me to be as bright-eyed and bushy-tailed as a ginger squirrel. We aren't all fortunate enough to be his long-lost god-daughters, you know."

"But *Tiggi*…" I implored, craving a second kiss.

"Never mind 'But Tiggi'. *BED!*"

6

O Welche Lust

Amid the stinky stenchy wet cigarette ends strewn across the damp concrete floor, against the cold hard blackened purple bricks of the bike-shed wall, we cuddled and kissed, kissed and cuddled, Tiggi clasping me vice-like beneath my burgundy blazer, me gripping her hips, relishing her bubblegum lips. I didn't care who knew, didn't care if the whole school knew. Oh! Proclaim our gayness to the town!

Then Charmian's vixen voice jolted us into wide-mouthed shock and stupor.

"Oh, yes. I've been waiting for weeks to catch you two at it. Straight to Miss Percival, girls. Now!"

And Charmian's face grew orange, furry, foxy, her purple 'Prefect' badge morphed into a collar, she fell on all fours and snapped, nipped nastily at our heels as we hastened trembling through the silent, studious quadrangle to our unjust justice, frantically, fearfully tugging at our high-rise panty lines, desperately dragging them down over our doomed behinds as we neared Miss Percival's lair. There she stood, auburn-maned and lilac-suited, firmly flexing her cane with an angry smile.

"Louise *Fawley*! Tiggi *Trebarwith*! Dis-*gusting*! Come into my office at *once*!"

I jumped, bolt upright and wide-eyed, gaping and gasping, palpitating and perspiring, to find myself in the cosy cane-proof comfort of my duck-down duvet in the sun-strewn Green Lady Room. Oh, thank heaven! Oh, that had been too real! Oh, Miss Percival! With auburn hair and lilac suit... Ohh...

Knock-knock-knock.

"Louise?"

Knock-knock-knock.

"Louise?"

Knock-knock-knock.

"LOUISE?"

"Tiggi!" My heart leaped with undisguised delight.

"For fuck's sake, get up! The commander's here! I have to start your induction in half an hour!"

"Oh, *please* come in, Tiggi-Wiggi! There's no need for *you* to knock!"

My bedroom door crept ajar and in slipped Tiggi,

attired in lemon polo shirt and cream cropped jeans. Her glorious hair slicked into a long lank ponytail, her beauteous face pallid with inch-thick slap, her sinuous sveltness noxious with flowery fragrance. I smirked in oh-so-knowing recognition. At Melusine Plastics, those of us who had harassed and hustled ourselves to our semi-somnolent desks for those sickening seven o'clock starts had nicknamed ourselves the Skunk Club – our sacred secret being to deny ourselves the refreshing decadence of morning showers, subservient instead to the sackcloth-and-ashes of slap and spray. Discovering in Tiggi a fellow Skunk endeared her to me even more. Had she emerged immaculate from her morning-after slumbers, I might have judged it nauseating near-perfection.

"Louise, I couldn't cadge some talc, could I? Pretty please? Once Chumleigh told me you were coming, I completely forgot to pop to the shop."

"Sure. In the pink holdall. There's a couple to choose from, I think. Help yourself."

Sliding onto my side, I hid my head beneath my blanket of down; down, nuzzling, snuggling into my pillow, longing to drink deep of Lethe again, desirous of devouring still more dreamy sleep.

"Oh no you don't!" Tiggi chided. "Up!"

And my soft feather-filled cocoon was wrenched from my bed.

"Bitch!" slipped from beneath my breath.

"*What* did you call me?" Tiggi demanded. "Onto your front, naughty girl, prepare to be spanked!"

A spanking! She wouldn't dare! Oh, please, please, let her dare!

And Tiggi grabbed my two big toes, one with each clenched fist, and twisted, twisted, the toe-twinge torture awful, angry. I pulled my pillows about me in last-gasp defence.

"Ow! Ow! Tiggi, please! You're hurting, hurting!"

Salvation came with a clatter as Rufus crashed through the bedroom door, his grey face a day dirtier, his silver stubble a sleep scruffier, his smouldering cigarette still sticking to his precipice lip.

"Morning, girls! A little something for your breakfasts, fresh filter coffee and hot bacon rolls. Hoho! I can see you're already playing at 'This Little Piggy', ha ha ha!"

After trashing our tray, brimming with coffee pots and mugs and saucers, crammed with crusty bacon rolls, onto a tiny side table, he was gone, bashing his way through the bedroom door as before.

"Shit!" I gasped, shocked. "Do you think he'll suspect?"

"Relax," soothed Tiggi, smiling as she released my feet. "He'll *know*, but won't whisper a word. I *promise*!"

My tormentor turned to the custard-coloured curtains, illuminated glorious golden by the burnishing summer sunshine. As she dragged the drapes asunder, the bright white light intensified tenfold. Reluctantly accepting the inevitability of morning, I keel-hauled myself from beneath my pillows, standing stupidly, sleepily, sloppily in my creased cream cami.

"Besides, your Uncle Charles would hardly hang us from the yardarm if it *did* come out."

An awkward pause ensued. When, only eighteen-odd short hours before, Gloria's beetroot head had risen like a rosy dawn from behind my sweet-dream duvet with a smiling, refreshing mug of sugary tea, the sole excitement enlivening my dreary diary had been Jade's promised prescription of yack-and-yarn and plum nail polish. Now, eighteen-odd short hours on, as Tiggi slipped her slender arms sensuously around me, hugging my hips, hooking herself tightly to me, I shone in sopping Sapphic serenity. Tears blurted from my hot salt eyes in release, in celebration, in relief, in confession.

"Oh, Tiggi!" I sobbed. "Thank you… Thank you… For the first time in my life I'm really me!"

"Hush, silly. Have you found the Maleffant Stumpwork?"

"The *what*?"

Unhanding my hips, Tiggi pulled at the dual doors of a tiny pine cupboard I'd mistaken for an ill-sited bathroom cabinet. Inside, not the commonplace array of menthol vapour rubs and morning-after pills, of toothpastes and tampons, of cough drops and condoms, but a hopelessly faded embroidery of clownishly clumpy figures and flowers. In their oranges and browns and greens, a gentleman with long locks, tight tunic and puff pants, and a gentlewoman all poodle perm and copious cleavage, bodiced and bumrolled, together held hands with impossibly long arms, while a bearded witch in a tall black hat and a charcoal cape hovered sombrely between them, the whole bordered by bouncing brown bunnies and pretty orange posies. Beneath a laser-printed paragraph laminated and mounted read:

> The Maleffant Stumpwork. Known to have been at Vetchley Castle since the Inventory of 1687, the work is traditionally accredited to Lady Amelia Maleffant, and is held to depict her sister Lady Arabella Maleffant, with her lover Nathaniel Llwyd; King Charles the Martyr looks down on the couple benignly. A captain in the Royalist infantry, Llwyd was killed at Naseby, on receiving which news Lady Arabella flung herself from the rooftops to her death. It will be noted that the figure of Lady Arabella holds her left hand to her abdomen; it is believed that she was carrying the unborn child of Nathaniel Llwyd.

"She was pregnant?" I stood staring, in tearful disbelief. "That's why she killed herself?"

"All disgrace and dishonour way back when, Louisey-Peasy. We've no idea how lucky we are to be free to choose as we please. We owe it to Lady Arabella Maleffant to live our lives as we like."

Oh, the bitch! The manipulative bitch!

Suddenly I felt so unsure. Oh, the secret, silent nights I'd snuggled deep into my oh-so-lonely bed after an alcohol-fuelled night on the town to fixate and fantasise on some shouty, pouty, barstool-bottomed party-popper I'd brazenly befriended, my imagination frantic to speed me to ecstatic rapture. But now, trapped in Tiggi's tentacle embrace, I didn't know. I just didn't know.

"Be in the commander's study in ten minutes, Louisey-Peasy. The other side of the Venetian Room."

Tiggi's lips pecked my neck. Then, pausing to grab her talcum powder and to help herself to a napkin-wrapped bacon buttie, she slipped through the slenderest crack of bedroom door.

Bewildered still by doubts and dreads, I hurriedly skunked up, cascading myself with dulcet droplets of enlivening eau de toilette, perfecting myself with tiny touches of pencil and powder, heaving my grey marl vest on over my creased cami, hauling my khaki shorts on over my lardy arse.

7

Captain on the Bridge

Down the dark, dingy, chocolate-coloured corridor I crept with mingling emotions, lust-pangs for Tiggi mixed with irritated ire at her attempt to slam-dunk me with her Lady Arabella Maleffant sob story. Tiggi Trebarwith, I'm no pushover. Don't you dare try to manipulate my heartstrings.

To my surprise, as I walked within earshot of Uncle Charles' study, I overheard Tiggi imploring, grovelling.

"Oh *please*, sir! *Please* don't leave me to Charmian! Oh *please*, can't you deal with me yourself?"

"Miss Trebarwith, I have placed minor disciplinary matters within the responsibility of Miss Mudher. You must answer to her on Tuesday, after the bank holiday."

"But she's already got me on a Verbal! She hates me! She'll give me a Written for sure!"

Tiggi was in trouble. I knocked softly on the dark oak door slightly ajar and pushed myself in past the brass plaque, COMMANDER CHARLES CHUMLEIGH, R.N., without waiting for the customary come-in.

"Well, well, well!" greeted Uncle Charles. "It would appear, Miss Trebarwith, that your wretched partner in profligacy has surfaced from her drunken slumbers!"

"Good morning, Uncle Charles."

"Is it, be damned? You are aware, Louise, that in your intoxicated states, you and your newly won friend succeeded in squandering a bottle of my very finest claret by reddening and ruining the Ponte Rialto fabric of one of our freshly reupholstered settees?"

"Oh, Uncle Charles! I'm so sorry!"

"And that your newly won friend is imploring me – in vain, I might add – to circumvent and override our normal disciplinary procedures, by attending to the matter myself, instead of leaving it to Miss Mudher, whose vengeance she dreads?"

"Oh, sir!" Tiggi implored. "*Please*, just this once! I'll pay for the upholstery to be cleaned!"

"Miss Trebarwith, procedures are procedures and must be adhered to, in our profession much more meticulously than in any other. At another time and in another place, your very life or the life of Miss Fawley here may depend upon your strict observance of our procedures and policies. No, Miss Mudher will attend to you when she returns on

Tuesday. Let *that* be *my* lesson to you."

In the sullen, sulky silence ensuing, I surveyed Uncle Charles' study. Its centrepiece was his chaotically cluttered desk, piled high with file upon file, some faded pink, some faded green, all bursting with ram-packed papers, all meticulously bundled with faded red ribbon, all arranged in slumping, slumbering stacks around the central blotting-papered workspace. More files in tottering, tumbling towers stood clumsily beneath and behind his giant desk, disguising a faded-to-beige rug with faintly discernible Chinese or Japanese fishermen freshly woven long, long ago. In places, the plank-like floorboards, blackened with age, stuck out like the ribs of a half-starved dog. Along one wall, an enormous, exquisite mahogany cabinet pressed into service as a library bulged with books on every subject – wines, warships, travel, theology, tennis, geography, gardening, cricket – while mounted opposite drooped a tired old map, Soviet Union and all, bristling with pins marking weapons of mass destruction long destroyed. Three stopped clocks purported to tell the times in New York, Moscow and Tokyo. Below berthed a handsome, homespun model of an old Leander-class frigate, its big-nosed bow perfect for ploughing the ever-restless, ever-rolling peaks and troughs of the North Atlantic.

And yet, even as the summer sunshine cascaded through the gorgeous Georgian windows, illuminating every dusty pile of papers, accentuating every neglected finger of furniture, the crazy disarray seemed, sunbeam by sunbeam, more and more to epitomise the eccentricities of omniscience, not dregs of decline and decay. The Cold War relics were a triumph, the closed files the cock-a-doodle-doos of victory. A demi-devoured bacon bap beside a lithe little laptop denoted Tiggi's desk, alongside that of the spiderlike spymaster. Nearby, on another tiny table, a beige electric kettle, orangey earthenware jars marked 'Coffee' and 'Sugar', and a plastic carton of blue-top milk strongly suggested that here was where the commander, Ahab-like, and his loyal-to-the-last lieutenant burned their investigative brain cells well into the silent, somnolent hours of one and two and three.

"However," continued Uncle Charles, levelling his fifteen-inch gun turrets towards me, "no self-imposed prohibition forbids me from intervening in the case of my own god-daughter, whose ambition, suffocated by excess wealth and a lamentable lack of self-discipline, has slumped to that of stealing a worthless childhood keepsake – a mug, for pity's sake – from her kindly former employer."

There was some truth in that.

"And now, it seems, even burglary isn't baseness enough for her, she stoops to wasting my wines!"

"I'm *so* sorry, Uncle Charles. I'll buy you a fresh bottle."

"A *fresh* bottle? A *fresh* bottle? Damn your eyes, girl, don't you see? The claret, girl, the claret! Your irresponsible hooliganism has robbed the world of a bottle of 2005 Château Diable! How the Devil do you propose to replace it? To travel back in time and tread a few more grapes? That blasted bottle you've squandered is irreplaceable! You might as well offer to paint me a fresh *Mona Lisa*!"

I felt stunned and scared, felt like a fearful schoolgirl, felt myself all but wet myself as Uncle Charles scolded. Rising from his round-backed, leather-backed old oak office chair he brandished a book at me, then proceeded to lecture me, pacing around and around me with slow, studied, measured steps.

"This," he tannoyed, "is my treasured, trusted copy of *Wines of the World* by no less an authority than the celebrated connoisseur Louis-Philippe Boileau-Champeaux. By great good fortune it has twenty-six chapters. For the next twelve months, each and every fortnight you will read, learn, and inwardly digest one chapter, at the end of which fortnight I shall test you. Should you fail to attain at least four out of five, you will repeat the chapter and test from the original French, *Vins du Monde*."

Uncle Charles peremptorily placed the admonishing volume into my dismayed hands. Tiggi, who had retreated behind her bacon bap, stifled her sniggers, mouthing, "LMAO!"

"Perhaps, Louise," he added, "by the time Miss Trebarwith has served the Written Warning, which I am sure she rightly anticipates, you will have derived a delicate appreciation for the arts of Bacchus."

For the first time in the longest time, I panged and pained with heartfelt contrition, warmly welcoming my chastisement. For the first time in the longest time, someone cared enough, loved enough to set me straight, instead of just nastily nagbagging me like my pernicious, pestilent mother, or simply dismissively deriding me like my smugly self-satisfied, obnoxiously self-obsessed ex-boyfriends.

"Sorry, Uncle Charles. I promise it won't happen again, Uncle Charles," I mumbled in a monotone.

"Now, if at last we might turn to the business of the day, perhaps you would kindly indulge me while I narrate my progress at the College of Arms yesterday, courtesy of my old friend Sir Nigel Naseby."

I seated myself, straddling a short stool, pinching a piece of stray bacon fallen from Tiggi's crusty bun.

"Before I arrived, Sir Nigel had telephoned his friends at *L'Ecole de la Noblesse Française* in Paris. It transpires that the family of de Leny de Longueville is an unblemished escutcheon, as loyal to the lilies as any of the old noble families of France. In 1204, Ranulph de Leny was among the first of the Norman baronage to side with King Philip on his march to wrench Normandy from our hapless King John. From those times onwards, at every battle from Bouvines to Dettingen, whenever history resonates with the clang and clamour of the century-on-century struggle between France and England, you'll find a de Leny sword-in-hand wrapped in the Fleur-de-Lys."

"Yes," I chomped, "Maurice de Leny was a real hero during the Second World War."

"*Louise!*" squealed Tiggi, "My *bacon!*"

"Our five principal suspects are five second cousins. Firstly, there is Richard de Leny, of Melusine Plastics, grandson of Maurice de Leny. Secondly, there are Léonard de Leny and Lionel de Leny, brothers. They are the grandsons of Maxime de Leny, who inherited Château de Longueville towards the end of the Second World War, in preference to his elder brother Maurice. Thirdly, we have Armand Lebrun and his sister Adolphine Lebrun, grandchildren of Marianne de Leny, the young sister of Maurice and Maxime, who married one Jean-Claude Lebrun, a captain in the Belgian army."

"I get it – I think."

"Now, as you both know, we have extensively – even exhaustively – examined the affairs of Richard de Leny and found damn all. Armand Lebrun occupies a dull-as-death finance position with some sort of manufacturer in Brussels. Adolphine Lebrun is a fitness instructress with her own gymnasium in a swanky suburb of Brussels. This all leaves me absolutely convinced that we'll find Léonard and Lionel de Leny behind La Ligne – whatever it means – which is why I'm packing you off to Sainte-Modeste-les-Colombes, where their elderly father Reynaud still lives in the family's clifftop villa."

"Lucky cow."

Uncle Charles beckoned me to his deskside where, hidden behind tottering towers of cluttering case files stood a cluster of three framed photographs. The first, most recent, labelled 'CCC RN WITH HM QE2' portrayed Uncle Charles resembling a plump pigeon in a light grey morning suit and pale pink waistcoat presented to Her Majesty the Queen, herself resplendent in luxuriant lilac hat and coat. The second, subtitled 'The Two Commander Chumleighs' depicted Uncle Charles as John Bull in a navy blue pinstripe suit and portly Union Jack waistcoat, with a tiny, aged, shrunk-to-nothing stalwart in a navy blue blazer rich with medals and bright white beret. The third, fuzzed and faded…the third was…the third was…Daddy, already ashen…and Uncle Charles, bearded, each in their naval uniform, at ease beside the sun-gold, tar-black stripes of HMS *Victory* – and there, nestling safely, securely, serenely, between them, a mini-Kylie – me! Oh, I dimly, dreamily remembered that sunny, happy day.

"Louise, it's perfectly possible that once you follow its scarlet thread through the labyrinth of Léonard and Lionel, you'll find that the trail of La Ligne leads straight to Richard de Leny. I must ask you – if such should prove to be the case – would you be capable of subordinating your loyalty to Richard de Leny, a man more like a father to you, and of rendering instead your suzerain loyalty to your Queen, whom you have never met?"

"I – I think so."

"You must know so, Louise. Remember, you may be called upon to betray Richard de Leny. Think long and hard upon that."

Third Movement

Modeste

1

Sur la Plage

The life of a secret agent was deadly dull. After the suave shaken-not-stirred sophistication of my first few evenings flirting and failing in the sleepy hotel bar, the rest of my fortnight loomed like gloomy-grey morning upon gloomy-grey morning, yawning on yawning. Four days into fifteen, I'd ticked through my holiday to-do list and was rabid with disappointment. Oh, I was bored…so sodding bored!

What was the point of priming me to identify de Lenys when there were no de Lenys to spot? Why stretch to the expense of giving me a flash spy tablet when I had nobody to spy on? What was I meant to do with my holiday wardrobe of Shane & Sheila essentials when there was no one to fall for my dishy disguises? I'd memorised the names and faces of every damned de Leny in the clan but none were in Sainte-Modeste. I'd systemised sending secrets to Godiva HQ but I had no secrets to send. I'd improvised flaunting myself in my Shane & Sheila collection but there wasn't a guy on the beach I'd fancy pumping me for false information.

The parish church of Sainte-Modeste had been dripping with lighted candles like the bean-bagged boudoir of an aromatherapy addict. Les Jardins des Mémoires had been creeping with nonagenarian Germans complaining that they should have won the war. La Place had been drooling with restaurants drunk on delectably divine cuisine, but on my beleaguered budget I could but tantalise my taste buds.

My character was Paula Godwin, a thirty-something hotel waitress from Southampton, who had just been made redundant and had chosen to waste her little windfall on a blow-away-the-cobwebs fortnight to redefine and rediscover herself. To my surprise, Paula's Scrapbook page was completely convincing, her leaving-do sleazily substantiated by plenty of photos of me amid my girl gang, lolling, laughing in my little black dress between a chunky-thighed pug in crop top and scarf-short skirt, and a vamping, vaping, blonde bitch in a skinny yellow dress with playing cards tattooed the length of her lily-white legs. Two best friends I'd never met. Where Tiggi had trawled them from, I didn't want to know.

In truth I'd found myself faulting Tiggi's judgement in many ways. Sainte-Modeste emerged as a gorgeously genteel relic of yesteryear, a tasteful, tranquil town, sweet and stylish; true *Douce France*. Most holidaymakers here were young French couples with pre-school children, escapees from the madcap hassle of Les Grandes Vacances, or elderly Germans on carefully chaperoned air-conditioned coach tours. Occasionally, backpacker Brits or Boks or Aussies or Kiwis bushwhacked their paths through the narrow hell-hot midday streets, lowering the tone and leaving me homesick, but generally I protruded like a mug of tea and a bacon buttie amid trayfuls of coffees and croissants.

I wriggled onto my front. Oh, what to do? When was the hotel beautician – Claudette – calling to do my nails? Tomorrow. Should I phone the spa and see if she could do this afternoon instead? I still fancied the idea of that deep plum colour; my emerald green was growing so shamefully chipped.

There was always *Wines of the World*…ugh! I felt a terrible tug of torture at the thought. So untrendy, so not the holiday read to be seen with, right in the middle of the beach. Worse, my head was already hurting in this horrid heat. If I opened that tome I'd become all nauseous and numbed. Surely it would be more sensible to save *Wines of the World* for later.

I dipped the tip of my tongue down into the drops and dregs of my vodka Martini, then reluctantly, resignedly condemned myself to the boredom of *Wines of the World*. Oh, the noxious notion of that catalogue of château upon château and vineyard next to vineyard and grape after grape! But better give it a half-arsed try, or Uncle Charles would roast my rump for sure.

The mesmerising sway of an accordion melody drifted down breeze-bound from the harbour heights. Thanks to Miles' eccentric, eclectic CD collection, I deciphered it as an arrangement of 'Il pleut dans mon coeur' and my mind's ear could hear the soothing, sonorous, balmy baritone of Georges Dubois:

Il pleut dans mon coeur
Mauvais et malheur
Vol est le voleur
Qui pillé sans peur.

The accomplished accordionist eased effortlessly into an arrangement of 'J'ai oublié mon chapeau'. Flaked, fatigued by the suffocating, scorching heat, I'd have gladly given a grand to feel a cooling English breeze licking my legs and fanning my back. Oh, *Wines of the World* or *EMD!* magazine? Hmm, decisions, decisions… Beneath a sea of gentle delirium I daydreamed at the beach scene before me…

Without doubt the crowning, anointing glory of any solemnity – whether wedding or wake, baptism or birthday – is the cake ceremony. That untouched, untasted centrepiece, its icing untrodden like freshly fallen snow, is presented with pride, its piping pristine, proclaiming coloured commemorations for congregational drooling, before all fall to carving and chomping. And yet, to my wide eyes, a more inviting delight is the sight of such a cake cut and demi-devoured, its geological striations of sponges and jams and marzipans and icings exposed to the weathering fingers of gorging, greedy me.

From my wriggle-bottom beach towel viewpoint, the ancient town of Sainte-Modeste-les-Colombes resembled such a semi-scoffed cake. On a scraggy, craggy clifftop surmounting the town, a dilapidated grey-stone château stood silent sentinel still above the jaunty jumble of scalloped terracotta roof tiles and prettily painted walls of La Ville Vieille, itself a layer above the strong, stern brown-stone walls of the high-tide harbour, bristling still with Louis-Quatorze gunports, now shelters for seagulls and perches for pigeons, all above sun-shimmering gingerbread sands and sun-sparkling chartreuse seas.

Oh my! Oh, wow! Oh, yes! An Adonis arose Aphrodite-like from the foam, gifted from the clean-green seas by Poseidon to the mortals of the sugar-brown sands. Lip-parting perfection! The seawater glistened on his bronzed body, running from his jet-black curls and his handsome head to accentuate every muscular curve of his brave biceps, proud pectorals, solid six-pack, taut thighs. Wrapped in wonder, I worshipped and wanted. Any guy looking spry in tiny turquoise budgie-smugglers was welcome to tick my box!

OMG! Could it be? From half a beach away, Mr Budgie-Smugglers had seen me, seized me, fixed on me, fixated on me, had loosened from his eyes tiny lust-darts straight into my eyes and down, deep down, penetrating my palpitating heart. Dripping with charisma, assuredly he strode from the sun-spangled sea, disregarding the happy, chatty, pelota-playing families, sidestepping the snoozing, slumbering, deckchair-dwelling pensioners, straight towards me!

My mock modesty mingling with mounting madness, my frenzied feelings feeding my carnal cravings, I hid my head half-heartedly behind the benignly smiling dust-cover portrait of Louis-Philippe Boileau-Champeaux on the back of my *Wines of the World*. Involuntarily, inexorably, my eyes gravitated, fascinated by that blue budgie, seemingly straining to writhe itself free from its tiny turquoise prison. Oh, far too many months had flown by since last a budgie had wriggled its way into me!

"*Aimez-vous les vins de France, mademoiselle?*"

Oh, heaven! I can't believe this is actually happening!

"Er…wee!"

"*Vous êtes anglaise?*"

Doh…is it that fucking obvious?

"Er…wee!"

"Me too. I'm from north-west London – well, Wembley. Dave Lanchbury…pleased to meet you."

OMG, he's English… Maybe this'll be one holiday romance I can pack in my suitcase and take home! "Lou—Paula Fawley – I mean, Godwin. Are you here on holiday?"

"No, I live in Sainte-Modeste. I'm a wine buyer for Pennypincher supermarkets."

Pennypincher! Léonard and Lionel de Leny sell to Pennypincher! Oh, I was getting warm!

"So, *do* you like French wines?"

"Oh, wee! I mean, yes!"

"Why not pop over to my apartment later? I've a dozen de Leny vins de table I'm dying to try. We could drink one or two with a bite to eat and watch the world go by. I've a great view of the harbour."

"Oh, I'd love to! Sounds divine!"

To my prying eye that budgie ever so slightly stiffened.

"Then it's a date… Seven o'clock?"

"Perfect!"

"Then, Paula, I'll look forward to seven. Come to 12 Rue les Pécheurs. Just ring my doorbell."

And away my Adonis strode, like Michelangelo's David made flesh. I marvelled at his beautiful scrammable back, his bountiful spankable buttocks, inching from that skimpy turquoise slip. Ohh!

What had Uncle Charles said? That the Château de Leny produced tolerable vins de table for Pennypincher! With luck, on one date, I could crack the code of La Ligne, and get amazingly laid. Oh, the life of a secret agent was far from deadly dull!

2

Baker Street

"Now *this* one," Dave explained, grabbing a clean plastic glass from the cardboard box at his sofa side, "is Le Chasseur Charmant, a bold red. We might decide to market it at the barbecue brigade."

"Coo!" I slurred. "Can you really target market that sisific…specific?"

"Sure. Les Moines de Cluny we'll promote as the classic companion to Sunday lunch, Chez Nous as the mood maker for romantic evenings in, Bienvenue as the party pleaser for any happy occasion."

"And this evening?" I teased. "Which of your wines is most appropriate to our little evening in?"

Dave was stunned into silence by my brazen bishop-to-queen-knight-five. Delighted with myself I rose, slinkily strolling, subtly swaying, flaunting my figure at the mild night air of the wide-open balcony. Again the well-remembered melody of 'J'ai oublié mon chapeau' dissolved into 'Les pigeons de Paris' drifting from a distant accordion as the reds and yellows and greens and blues of the pretty harbour lights illuminated here and there the prow of a yacht or a lobster pot or a canoodling quayside couple.

Our evening had been divine diversion. After four practically Trappist days confined by oui and non and parlez-vous, it had been honeyed heaven to converse, to chatter, to charm and be charmed, to stoop to flirty and dirty anglais to anglaise. But disappointingly, Dave Lanchbury definitely had nothing to declare. He was honest, hard-grafting, clean-cut and clear-cut, the representative of Pennypincher supermarkets he had always purported to be. But far from having an angle on La Ligne, he was barely acquainted with Léonard and Lionel de Leny, for all he commandeered their vintages by the barrel.

"What's on your mind?" he quizzed, thoughtfully, touchingly, as he rose and strode close behind me.

Well, I've given it my best shot, Uncle Charles, I mused. The rest of the evening is mine.

"Oh, *Dave!*" I gasped breathlessly, yieldingly, achingly, letting my head fall against his statuesque chest, nuzzling, snuggling. "*Dave!*" My tiny lithe fingers loosened the tantalising buttons of his ice-white Oxford-cotton shirt, facilitating the sensuous, stroking ingress of my inquisitive digits over those manly mammaries.

Dave huddled my waist with his rugby scrum arms, then…ohh! His tingling tongue tickled my earlobe, transmitting inescapable, irresistible paralyses of pleasure coursing my helpless, hapless body, and…ohh, again!… and ohh, again! Those electric ecstasies moistened me and maddened me in mingling moments…ohh, so not fair! Ohh, so not fair! He'd hit upon my Ardennes and had punched his panzers through. My defences were down and my knickers were next. All that was left was surrender…

"*Fuck* me! *Now*!" I breathed. "Just *do* it!" I gasped. "*Please*!"

I arched my aching, anticipating legs wider, wider; bending over the balcony giddier, giddier; presenting myself to my conqueror, my commander. Deftly, Dave tucked my skirt up into my waistband, yielding a tingling thrill transporting me through time to the dread and dire discomfort of Miss Percival's bend-over desk. Then, *Oh My Gosh*! As Dave slid into me I supposed his massive manhood had poked a hole through my skimpy, sopping knickers to fill me, fulfil me… *Oh My Gosh*! Like a mighty powerful piston sliding slowly to and fro and in and out… *OH MY GOSH*! Again I arched my aching legs wider, wider, to capture his pumping pangs of pleasure deeper, deeper.

The first shock of penetration passing, I collected my composure, resolving to give this big bad boy a taste of my talked-about tenacity, to grind him to his knees between my millstones. Gently I gripped him, initiating my slinky sway to souse his soft spot, holding him taut and tight; but *ohh* he hit my magical, mystical oh-zone; *ohhh* again, *ohhhh* again; impossible to dissemble my indelible delirium…

"Yeoww! Yeoww! Yeoww!" I moaned and groaned in tones half-female, half-feline, at once delighted and defeated, at once exhilarated and humiliated. "Yeoww! Yeoww! Yeoww!"

Sensing my ecstasy, Dave prodded and prodded at my pleasure patch, each stroke stronger and stronger, until in spite of myself I began to catch. Oh, NO! Already I was past the point of no return…

And now, from deep, deep within me, my orgasm bubbled and boiled, tangy tingling mingling with marvellous majestic indescribable delight, heavenly pleasure crescending and cascading, slowing to simmering, transcending all space and time with sizzling sensations, steeped in out-of-body serenities.

"OH! OH! OH!" I exhaled, sending spurting skyward five white doves, refugees from the eaves above, up, up, up into the inky-blue star-strewn sky, all fright and flap and feathers.

"Oh, fucking hell!" I panted, exhausted, near-nauseous with numbness. "Oh, *Dave*, that was *divine*!"

"Bakerloo Line?" he breathed into my ear in baritone.

Oh no, *please*! How the heck could he want *more*? Surely he'd already come *once*. And now *anal*? About as much fun as kissing cardboard. My arse would ache for days and I wouldn't poo properly for a fortnight. I grimaced, gritting my teeth and allowing my eyes to mesmerise to the dancing dabs of reds and blues and greens and yellows all waltzing with waves of inky-black as the evening tide ebbed gently. I relaxed myself to receive his big push... I'd see my playmate nursing a knackered knob yet.

"Go for it," I deadpanned in granite tones. "Lube me up."

Dave's deft, darting, tickling fingers reconnoitred the attack ahead of his penetrating column, undefeated, unstoppable, uncomfortable, buggering my butt muscles inch by inch and thrust by thrust. Then...miraculously...I sensed that Dave was struggling to hold his load...I worked and worked him, squeezed and squeezed him, the stubborn shit and ohh...with a lion-like roar he discharged his scalding spurt and...withdrew like a cork from a bottle! Oh, *yes*! Fawley's fabled record stood intact!

As I panted, palpitated, and at length permitted my heart rate to calm and my breathing to ease, Sainte-Modeste-les-Colombes seemed to be drifting out to sea and drifting off to sleep along with the night-time tide. The accordion players silenced by the softness of the night, the harbour largely plunged into tar-black darkness, the only sounds the occasional chinks of wine glasses accompanying tranquil ripples of party laughter. Oh, how I hoped my own moans and grunts and groans had not carried on the still night air!

I turned to confront the masculine mayhem of the awfully arrayed apartment. Dave himself had crashed, bare-legged and bare-bottomed, face down over his sofa, his ice-white shirt sweat-patched and creased, his crumpled cartoon boxers carpeted, his trousers heaven alone knows where. *Men*!

To gatecrash the stale unwholesome bedroom of a man oblivious to all seemed as sacrilegious as stealing and plundering a way into the hallowed tomb of an afterlife-awaiting pharaoh. Instead, the homely spare room with its dainty divan and strawberry-strewn bedspread led me on. Strangely swimmingly wantonly weary, stumbling and staggering…as far as…ohh…my head hurt…as far as…giddy…giddy…giddy…ohh…falling into softness…ohh such softness…snuggling…snuggling…ohh!

3

CREDO

Even before that little Kylie-like me had tugged at the gold braid cuffs of those two Hearts of Oak alongside the wooden walls of HMS *Victory*, I had deeply, devoutly, instinctively, imploringly, adoringly believed. To me, that God is, always has been, ever shall be, that all-embracing, all-empowering, ever-evolving, ever-expanding Love, binding all Creation into One, comes as easily as breathing, is as crystal clear as the cosmic blue skies. What else would you have me believe? That the Universe and everything in it sprang into existence within a fraction of a second in one ginormous Big Bang? How ridiculous! But a living, loving, infinite, indefinite Creator, sculpting and smoothing the rude ragged rocks, calming and caressing the madness of matter, breathing love and life into the quasars and pulsars of far-flung space as into the fishes of the deep and the fowls of the air on our own spiral-arm backwatered Planet Earth – *that* I believe. And Heaven? The Realm of God? I imagine it's a sort of Parallel Universe, separated from ours by a heartbeat, from which God, immortal, invisible, perpetually perceives and patiently persuades, omniscient therefore omnipotent; and into which we, as through a glass darkly, occasionally gain glimpses and insights into Him.

Hence when, from the sweetest of sleeps, the most delectable of dreams, I softly, slowly felt myself aroused and awakened by a roundly resonant church bell – tolling… tolling…tolling – and divined that it was Sunday, my heart leaped resplendent with joy and I lay, wide-eyed, wide awake, widely smiling.

My mind entwined in morning-after numbness, I wallowed in my wanton weariness, relishing my freshly-fucked feeling, savouring my serene soreness. A deadening, leadening, paralysing pain smarted my arse; with each merest movement came agonising ache. But what did I care? These were wounds earned on the battlefield of love, each painful pang a memorable favour or fancy. Again I read the little love note which Dave had secreted beneath my dreaming, designing, delighting pillow:

> *Hi Paula, I hope by the time you read this you'll have enjoyed a lovely long sleep. You're in the room my sister Sarah uses whenever she visits me in Sainte-Modeste and*

she always finds it a pleasantly restful room. Alas – cruelly – I've been summoned by email back to Pennypincher Head Office in Cheltenham for a week of meetings but please, please, stay in my apartment as long as you like, treat my place like your own home. If I'm really lucky you'll still be here when I get back and we can explore the sights and restaurants of Sainte-Modeste together. Please feel free to help yourself to anything – Sarah's clothes will suit you perfectly and save you a stroll back to your hotel. Please think of me suffering in my shirt and tie in those interminable stuffy meetings. Missing you already. David. xxxxx

In my semi-somnolent state, I had counted church chimes summoning me from my soothing slumbers ten…eleven…twelve…and now, as I eavesdropped on the footfall and clatter and laughter and chatter of the hither-and-thither tourists and townsfolk in the tiny windy stone streets below, an amorous accordion resumed its melodic, mesmeric rise-and-fall with 'Le Clair de La Lune' and I hugged Dave's little missive to my happy, happy heart. Oh, it could only be love! Oh, I'd known it from that magical moment when Dave arose Adonis-like from the foam! Oh, read and see! *'Please stay in my apartment as long as you like'* and *'treat my place like your own home'* and *'if I'm really lucky you'll still be here when I get back'* and *'help yourself to anything'* and conclusively *'Sarah's clothes will suit you perfectly'*. Oh, that was a slice of Sigmund surely! No loving brother could couple his sweet sister in the same sentence with any other woman unless he perceived them as somehow similar, and longed for their lifelong friendship. Surely Sarah was Georgiana Darcy and I Elizabeth Bennet – except this was 2018 and Pemberley was mine – well, Kimberley anyway – with Gwynfor and Gloria thrown in as a job lot…

Thoughtfully, tidily, Dave had placed my bag beside my bed, so, braving my aching arse I stretched and grabbed my tablet, dextrously delving onto my Scrapbook page. Tiggi – alias Pixie – had posted a selfie gorging a Cornish pasty, captioned 'Enjoying a few days unexpected leave', while Charmian – simply Char – teased me 'Got yourself a guy yet?' This was the predetermined code for 'Any luck with La Ligne?' But perplexingly it came from Char not Pixie. Oh, Louise! Wasn't it obvious? Charmian had sacked Tiggi from mentoring me! Oh, the big bad bitch! Well, she wouldn't get her flabby fat arse one rotten rung up her career ladder courtesy of me! Smirking, slyly I replied, 'Not a sausage!', reminiscing randily on my ravishing rendered by Dave's great Cumberland curl sizzling and spurting within me.

I tried to think things through. Maybe Dave *was* barely on nodding and bobbing terms with Léonard and Lionel de Leny, but postcard-perfect Sainte-Modeste had been his home for nine fine years and he knew every curve, every courtyard of the cantankerous old contour-clinging town. Its preservation in 1930s aspic it owed to a triumvirate of landlords, namely, the Famille de Leny, of old blood and new wines; the Convent of Sainte-Modeste, in orchard-and-vineyard seclusion on the northerly outskirts of town; and the Famille Bouchard, whose industrious, industrialising forebears had landed a fabulous family fortune in pickled fish. Add to the gentle wealth of these three estates the drive and determination of local lad Jean-Pierre Blanquer, a leader of the wartime Maquis who, having helped liberate his homeland from the Nazis with fighting and sniping, spent the next four decades defending his home town by democratic means from every architect and bureaucrat and contractor and developer that the post-war world could hurl against its lovely crumbly walls. Yes, I felt let down to learn that all the artful accordionists were on the payroll of the Hôtel de Ville, that their seemingly spontaneous repertoires were in fact carefully choreographed, that even the terracotta pots of gorgeous geraniums lovingly watered by hoteliers and householders alike were provided by the town. But as Dave told me, I had only to rove to Sainte-Monique next on the coast, languishing alongside a horrid hedgehog of high-rise hotels in drab dull concrete, littering the coastline like leftover world war tank traps, to imagine the disfigured, brutalist portrait hidden out of sight by Sainte-Modeste in her garret attic.

And yet the mystery of La Ligne had seemingly deepened and darkened. It transpired that, back at the start of the summer, the near eighty-five-year-old Reynaud de Leny had suffered a slight stroke, leading his loving sons Léonard and Lionel to shepherd him to their own seaside villa to ensure his perpetual care. Villa de Leny they had leased to their second cousin Armand Lebrun who had high-minded ideas of launching some sort of refugee relief project. But so far his only practical act had been to install a new housekeeper, so devilish and so deranged, that one by one the trusted staff of old Reynaud de Leny had quit their positions. Now no one from Saint-Modeste would take a place there. Even for an evening's entertaining, chefs and sous-chefs and waitresses had to be trawled in from Toulon.

But the most arcane revelation concerned Marianne de Leny and Jean-Claude Lebrun. Dave had explained that they had not married until 1946, as Jean-Claude, a captain in the courageous Belgian army, had paced up and down throughout the hostilities hutched in a Wehrmacht prisoner-of-war camp. Georges Lebrun was in fact their adopted son, a boy found wandering Longueville, frightened and friendless amid the chaos of May 1940, and sheltered in Château de Leny by Marianne. So neither Armand nor Adolphine were truly of de Leny descent. Neither Armand nor Adolphine could lay any claim to – nor play any part in – La Ligne, whatever the Devil it might mean. So for me to be squandering a summer in Sainte-Modeste-les-Colombes, laying one-woman siege to a *Villa de Leny* without a de Leny inside it was perfectly pointless. One fact was obvious. Tiggi had goofed. Tiggi had blundered. Tiggi was an absolute arse. No wonder Charmian had sacked her. Tiggi Trebarwith – pah!

FUCK! My heart hastened to double time as telltale squeaking and creaking heralded heaven knows who through Dave's apartment door, and a Lancashire lass cheerily, cheekily called "Hiya, Dave! Are y'in, love?" SHIT! Another girlfriend! For sure she's going to bawl at me, bitch at me, scram me, slap me, sling me into the street, headache and heartache and arse ache and all! Oh, the two-timing turd!

4

JOANNE

A maddening mingling of emotions muddled and muddied my mind. Foremost, fear; fear at my imminent, inevitable, detection; fear at what green-envy, girly-slap reprisals this no-nonsense northern soul might make; fear at my own panging paralysis, my arse ache anchoring me to my borrowed bed like some skewered suckling. Secondly, heartbreaking, harrowing, howling, hurt, burning and bubbling at treacherous, two-timing Dave. My stinging, scalding tears plopped onto the tissue-of-lies pallid-blue airmail paper he had scandalised with his billet-doux, dissolving its falsehoods like acid as I coughed and choked on my own smashed and scattered true-love fantasies.

"Sarah?" quizzed the interloping intruder, "are y'in, love?"

I sensed my love rival right behind me. Oh, please, please, please, let her be forgiving!

"Oops, sorry, love! You must be Dave's latest piece o stuff! I'm Joanne, friend and neighbour."

Joanne, friend and neighbour? Thank you! Thank you! Thank you!

"Hi Joanne, I'm Paula, Dave's new girlfriend," I rebounded, relieved and reprieved, greedily grasping my night-into-noon acquittal. "Excuse me if I don't get up, but I'm a little bit worse for wear this morning. Both barrels, if you know what I mean. Men!"

"Girlfriend?" cackled Joanne, wryly and slyly. "Good luck wi that one, love!"

Joanne slowly strode the length of my bed, perching her pert behind beside my plump pillow. Thirtyish, tallish, lithe, lissom, with luxuriant bronze-blonde lob, gingerbread-brown skin, and dreamy, dopey features set with the sleepiest, serenest of smiles and two huge emerald eyes. Her scrumptious oatmeal dress decked with the prettiest of prints, dainty daisies of forget-me-not blue; her smooth, sculptured, tightly crossed legs led to fresh cream pumps, fastened with turquoise laces.

"A little bit sore, are we, love? Get somewhere water can't, did he?"

The herald of humiliation hollered. Oh, please don't tell me anal is Dave's party piece!

"Pinched your knickers too, I'll bet?"

OMG! They were gone! Maybe I'd dropped them off before getting into bed. Oh, please don't tell me Dave's a knicker-nicker!

"Dave isn't like that," I protested. "We've got something special. Already. See? Read his letter!"

Deeply darkly Davy Jones drowning, desperate for a lifeline, I proffered Joanne Dave's love-soaked letter, cringing, crying, expecting a debacle of derision. Instead, an inquisitive, interested, intentness spread the breadth of Joanne's earnest, honest face. At length she sighed, smiled, and said, "Well! I've never known im talk to a woman in that fashion before! If I didn't recognise is writin I'd swear it weren't im what wrote it. Perhaps e as seen somethin in ya. What e needs after all is a good woman. Stuck down ere on is own, making too much money, all those gorgeous girls on t' beach, all after holiday rumpy-pumpy. Temptation's been too great for im. Aye, a good steady woman. An' you could be't one, Paula. I like ya. Tell ya what, I'll go n make us a lovely brew."

All those gorgeous girls on the beach, all after holiday rumpy-pumpy? Temptation's been too great for him? Ohh! Dave Lanchbury, just you wait!

"So, what *are* ya doin down ere, Paula? What d'you do for a livin?"

I deadpanned my secret service falsehoods, abashed and awkward trying my lying on sugar-sweet Jo.

"I'm a hotel waitress. I've just been made redundant. I've come away to rediscover myself."

"Then you've fallen on your feet, love. *Stay.* You've

already moved in wi im, as good as. There's always plenty o work in San Modeste for good waitresses in't otels, specially ones what can speak good English. An you n me'll become't best o friends. Oh, *stay*, Paula! I'll make us that brew!"

"And what brought *you* to Sainte-Modeste, Jo? You don't strike me as the holiday rumpy-pumpy sort?"

"It were mi sister. Laura. She were backpackin along't coast ere three year ago, just disappeared, completely disappeared. San Modeste were't last place she were seen. I came ere, lookin for clues, lookin for anythin, but found nothin. Vowed to stay till I found er. Three year on, I'm still ere."

"Oh, Joanne!" I consoled. "I'm so sorry. I'm so, so sorry!"

"Well, mi French isn't up to much and I didn't ave much luck oldin down a job. So I took up mi old obby o paintin. Beach n't arbour most o't time. Or't streets n squares. They're not much for't look at, mi paintins, but tourists love em. They'll sell for anythin up to two hundred euro a piece. Between them n Dave's Pennypincher freebies, I more than get by."

For a few mesmeric moments my mind wandered and wondered in a stare-at-the-stars sort of way. Life seemed to be a country dance of hellos-and-goodbyes, hellos-and-goodbyes, amid the clapping and the stamping and the fiddling and the reeling never dreaming in the thick of giddy roundelay that our next link of arms may prove our last. My remembrance flickered dimly back to my last stolen look at my father, in ashen bedridden agony begging my mother, "Please don't let the girls see me like this, Jean." My thoughts tunnelled to Tiggi, salt tears streaming across her cute cheeks as she relived and recounted that awful afternoon her parents' *Petroc* smashed to shards on the ragged rocks…

"I'll make us that brew. An I'll see if Dave's got some Painfen tablets knockin' about. Tell ya what, I'm plannin on poppin over to San Monique later for a few bevvies, gettin a taxi in. Fancy comin?"

Sainte-Monique? Dave had already warned me it was all concrete and couscous and chips, but wait…

"Yawwn!" I hammed. "Yawwn! Let's save it til I'm more myself. But, the Sainte-Monique road, isn't that the one heading straight up the hill out of town, then bending inland alongside the Villa de Leny?"

"Aye, that's the one," affirmed Joanne. "Rue des Pécheurs becomes Rue de Leny just outside ere."

"Jo, would you mind if I shared your taxi, as far as Les Jardins des Mémoires? I simply adore the view of Sainte-Modeste from there. At least I'll have wrenched something from this dreadful day."

"You've already got somethin out o't day, y'cheeky cow, you've met me! Your new lifelong friend! Of course we can share't taxi. An I'll make us that brew."

5

Mistook

Scant wonder the war-weary Wehrmacht vainly entrenched their enfilade of ship-shattering, invasion-impounding, big-booming great guns here, commanding a perfectly parabolic seascape stretching too blue to be true from 240 East to 100 West, surveying a shimmering skyline where azure air met sapphire sea. Nowadays, Les Jardins des Mémoires occupied the outcrop, and convalescents not conscripts breathed the fragrant flowers of peace, not the choking cordite of war. A burnished bronze sculpture perpetuated for posterity the surrender without a single shot of mannered Major von Kremp and his ambivalent *Artilleristen* to jaunty Jacques Blanquer and his jubilant Maquis.

Joanne slammed shut her taxi door, blew me a big kiss in au revoir, then Stavros sped her away, with wheelspin, dust and dirt. All alone in the silent, sandy square where Villa de Leny proffered an uninviting, uninspiring, grim grey lie of a crumbling concrete wall to a money-hungry world, I half-hobbled, half-halted, wimping and wincing, towards Les Jardins, savouring the softness of a gentle zephyr, and the potpourri of exciting, enticing, lingering scents from the sweet-as-Eden gardens.

It seemed impossibly strange. Paula Godwin had ventured to Sainte-Modeste to rediscover and reinvent herself, but enjoying an epiphany had fallen to Louise Fawley. From the vantage point vacated by those long-vanished 340-millimetre monsters, lolling languidly, lazily even, in Sarah's flouncy frock of strawberry prints, titillating to the sweet breeze caressing my legs, dozily daydreaming down on that loveable, huggable lopsided town, to me Sainte-Modeste resembled a gorgeous, generous Battenberg slice, slipping into a tea-green sea, her harlequin buildings in ochres of yellows and pinks and creams and browns seemingly squares of softest sponge. There close to the Old Harbour hid the window where last night I'd been truly torpedoed below the waterline. Hypnotised by the gently bobbing boats and the ever-transient palette of reflected dabs of light and life, I longed to bob with Dave in the rippling sea-green sheets of his bull-run bachelor bed.

As that shimmering, seemingly simmering sea stretched to the convex curve defining, delineating our plucky planet, so my renaissance, my resurgence beckoned me, beguiled me into the infinite, the indefinite; towards the exhilaration, the expectation of the whole of the rest of my life. Could I start to simply shake away those dreadful hateful hurtful decades, to curl my lip at Mother's bitchy beastly wounding words, to shrug off Miss Percival's depraving paining canings, to flash two fingers at that junta of jokers, Giles and Miles and James? I pictured winter in Sainte-Modeste, the bare beaches bereft, the sodden skies slate-grey, with Mr and Mrs Lanchbury-to-be, wedding-wrapped in anoraks and arrans, cuddling and canoodling their way all along the lobster-potted breakwater walk. I imagined Christmas Day, the tiny, tidy red-gingham-curtained kitchen corner of our lust-nest heavy with sprout-scented steam as Joanne wrestled with vegetables and Dave sliced the so-soft sweetly succulent turkey and I popped open chilled champagne as the Queen streamed from Sandringham.

Staring seaward to the glimmering, glistening ever-twinkling waves, it hit me as cringingly cruel that this could possibly be the same shifting sea where, so my sensationalise-and-terrorise television news told me, this vicious, vindictive morning some dozen luckless migrants had drowned to their deaths when their rickety ship, groaning to the gunwales, decks awash with dreams, holds loaded with hopes, had suddenly splintered amidships and sunk. From six hundred kilometres south by south-south-east their agonised anguish rippled palpably, painfully, sending shivers and shudders snaking my spine.

Innocently, indifferently, happy holiday hubbub drifted dulcet up from the carefree carnival beach, loudest that of the Sainte-Modeste Town Band, sounding a riotous, raucous crashing, clashing of brash brass and pom-pom-pom percussion. The madcap medley of delirious discord was decipherable as another adorable Georges Dubois classic. I serenaded myself with its jaunty, jolly let's-party lyrics:

> *Vivienne et Véronique*
> *Elles caqetent comme les cacatoès*
> *Sensuelles et sympathiques*
> *Chaque nuit elles dansent Le Bongo*

My swinging sunset bubble was burst in an instant by an insistent, intrusive tug at my arm, as a short and swarthy termagant with long lank black bob and brown beady piggy eyes and lardy lumps languishing in her horrid hessian dress harassed and harangued me with frantic, frightful frowns.

"You are the waitress of the silver service? *Oui*? You are the waitress of the silver service?"

Instantly flipping into MI69 mode, rapidly retrieving my hotel helpmate *alter ego*, I replied, "Err…wee!"

"Your *voiture*, she has fallen into *panne*? *Oui*? You are arrived in the taxi, *maintenant*?"

"Err…"

That couldn't be right! Paula Godwin didn't own a *voiture*!

"*Vite! Vite!* Already you are in *retard*! *Habillez-vous*! Michelle will show-*ez vous*! Michelle! Michelle!"

A pretty, pouty, waif-like, wench-like twenty-something

appeared, scurrying, hurrying from the grey gates of Villa de Leny before standing still, legs together and hands clasped, dreading yet defying, like a summoned schoolgirl. Her blonde, tangled, tousled, tresses battled with her prim, trim waitress-wear of sloe-black dress and snow-white apron with white-as-ice thigh-highs and black-as-night slip-ons. Her hemline so short, the merest millimetre from vertical would risk a cheeky peek.

"Oui, Madame?"

"*Montrez-vous la bête anglaise son uniforme!*"

"Oui, Madame!"

And Madame angrily grabbed my fearful forearm with her horrid, hairy hand, hauling me hellward through the dread doors of Villa de Leny like some sacrificial sheep to my diabolical doom.

"Madame! Jer vooz on pree! Jer ner swee paa een serverze!"

"*Silence, salope! Dépêchez-vous! Habillez-vous! Vite! Vite!*"

6

Unjust Desserts

Madame harangued and harassed me across the stark yard of cream concrete and chalk chippings, occupied by two smart saloon-cars in totalitarian black – a Brandenburg 800 and a Bayern B6, I thought – before pointing and pushing me through a slam-shut dungeon door into a dingy, dirty, vaulted, vestry-like chamber, dripping with corbels and cobwebs, lit only by apertures like arrow slits.

"Madame!" I wailed in vain, tearfully thumping the old oak gaoler.

Michelle moodily, morosely lolled and laughed alongside an ancient chestnut bench the length of the old peeled whitewashed wall encrusted with heavy hooks of black iron.

"She is *la bitche*," badmouthed Michelle. "But where else in Sainte-Modeste can you gain fifteen euro par hour in travail as the waitress?"

From one hook hung pristine-clean waitress-wear in a zip-up suit-bag labelled 'Jessica Jenkins'.

"Jessica, we ave ere your sizes you tell us. Dress *vite vite* or we will ave both *la gronderie*."

Jessica Jenkins! Another alias! I mused melancholically, even mournfully, down at Sarah's summer sunshine designer dress of strawberry prints. Just as I'd succeeded in slipping into something special…

"Also make attention for *La Perruche*, she is *la fille du Diable*. She is the poodle of Madame."

And yet, perhaps I would claw good from this. Little could my captors guess they had pressed an agent of MI69 into their service. Maybe I'd wander at will through Villa de Leny, squirrelling secrets…

"I return in five minutes. Make ready!"

And Michelle deserted me through a cunningly concealed door at the darkened end of the vestry, the bright light beyond momentarily framing her egress, the gothic vault reverting to its gloomy greyness.

Reluctantly stepping from Sarah's scarlet shoes, resignedly unbuttoning myself from her gorgeous genuine *Gigi Giselle*, hanging it half-heartedly from a rough, rude ferrous peg on the cold clammy wall, I delved deep into Jessica's suit-bag. Hm, black top, black skirt, black pumps, white thigh-highs…

"Ee! Ee!" squeaked something from somewhere. A rat? A bat? Shit! Quick! Change, Louise, change!

Hauling the top down over my head, tidying my tangled mop as best as poss, flamingo-like I smoothed the sensuous thigh-highs up the lengths of my legs, their elasticated tops caressing my chubby calves. Next I slipped the skirt on but, oh, it was so shit-small! Standing legs together I could scarcely writhe and wriggle its waistband up over my big broad bottom – three times I zipped it tightly only to hear and feel the zip rip apart again. At last, raising it ensign-high, breathing in and breathing in, I succeeded in stretching and straining it shut around the least podgy portion of my waistline. Finally, I squeezed my feet into the black pumps, and tied the bright white apron around me, just as Michelle crashed back through her cat flap.

"You are *habillée*? Ohh, you English girls! Ohh, there is no time! *Ohh, eh bien, on doit faire avec!*"

Now it fell to Michelle to wrest my wrist as she dragged me dumbed through the gloomy vestry door into a long, light, bright white cloister-like corridor with lumpy, bumpy walls set with pinky-grey glistening-granite casements. At an old dark oak dresser bejewelled with bountiful brûlées of chocolates and caramels and creams she paused and pouted at its black-blotted, lacklustre mirror.

"Already they ave eaten the *plat principal*. At each time the Monsieur Armand e make the discourse before the *dessert*. When e as terminate is discourse, they applauds, we serve the *dessert*. *Oui?*"

"Err…wee!"

"*Bien.* You attend ere. *Je dois faire un pipi.*"

I looked like a moulting magpie next to the perfectly

preened Michelle! I tried to tidy my tangled tresses, but in this little pulchritude pageant I was definitely second best. I sighed and shrugged. Then, from an adjacent double-doorway framed with sparkling stone like that of the pinky-grey crystalline casements came the angsty, angry, argumentative phlegm of someone spouting some sort of speech.

"They hate us because they know that we are right. They hate us because might is right. They hate us because they know how close the glorious Third Reich came to triumph on every front. They hate us because they fear the inevitable certain victory of our glorious Fourth Reich that is to come."

Third Reich? Fourth Reich? What the hell was this guy on?

"Our new five-footed swastika seals our determination to stamp our vision on all five continents of this corrupted world. Nothing – neither nation, nor notion – will prevent us. The muddle-minded Brussels bureaucrats will learn that legislation is powerless against armies. The brainless British will discover that their Brexit is not a Royal Air Force that can take to the skies to defend them. The decadent and divisive United States will find itself friendless amid our glorious New World Order."

Several shouts of "Sieg Heil!" shot semi-spontaneously from an ambient audience.

"In every nation of Europe the True Right is on the march once more. We must unite and unify these virtuous, natural passions of the people, channelling their streams of white-hot anger to forge a sword worthy of Siegfried's wielding, a sword hungry for a vicious vengeance. We must…"

Could this be La Ligne? Could dear old Meanie de Leny really be mixed up with this lot? New Nazis! It was incredible, impossible! And yet, if only I could sneak and stretch and see…

"…the Eagles of Death will awaken from their shameful slumbers…"

A sudden, searing, tearing, twinge racked my rogered rear. I staggered sideways, my backside bashing the old oak dresser, a clownish clattering and crashing ensuing as brûlée after brûlée toppled from the table. Hurriedly, hastily, bending, reaching to rescue them, I found myself facing the feet of Madame.

"*Imbécile!*" squealed Madame. "*Bitche anglaise!*" And hauling me howling hellward by my hurting head of hair, she screamed, "For you, there is no Jesus Christ! For you, there is no Oly Mother! For you, there is only Madame! For you, there is only *la vaisselle!*"

Tiles upon tiles of terracotta paved my ignominious procession to a big butcher-block table piled impossibly high with dozens of dirty dishes.

Surveying my surroundings, I'd been Shanghaied to the most antediluvian, antique scullery I had seen, save for those pickled for posterity by British Heritage. Two huge white-glazed earthenware sinks, that on the left brimming with steamy, soapy water, that on the right millpond-still with calm, clear water, were flanked by work-worn wooden drainers, sloped and smoothed by years upon years of servitude. From yukky-yellow walls lurched rickety crockery racks, things of torture not devices of domesticity.

"Every glass, every knife, every plate you will *faire la vaisselle*!" snarled Madame, brandishing an example of each in turn, then setting her seal on my incarceration with an expletive slam-shut exit.

Feeling depressed and diminished, I sank and shrank before that threatening precipice of crockery and cutlery, those lukewarm leftovers from a revolting reeking fish dish, some sort of stew bobbing and bogging like turds in a tureen. And yet, my venture into Villa de Leny had proven instructive and informative. I now knew that La Ligne led to nothing more nasty or narcotic than a brainless, badass bunch of nutcase New Nazis, a silly, society-swanking set who would probably prioritise canapés before dinner over guns before butter. A five-footed swastika? Oh, please! They'd be derided from Donegal to the Dardanelles! Oh, Uncle Charles would be so pleased with me when I told him! All I needed now was to serve my shift in the style of the ignorant little bitch Madame believed me to be, then skedaddle back to the safety and security of Dave's harbourside haven…my future matrimonial home!

Without doubt the most miserable, menial task can bask in glorious, golden gaiety, if only we party-plunge into the spirit and swing of the thing. I determined to throw my own little kitchen knees-up, a champagne celebration for unearthing and unravelling La Ligne. The glassware first – dregs of demi-sec blanc I downed as I danced, round and round, *tout en rond*, sploshing and splashing each glass in the soapy sink as I made a maypole of the great greasy pile of dirty dinnerware. Then – mmmm...ohhh...*orgasme de la bouche* – a divinely inspired chicken dish, succulent cutlets oozing with sensational stuffing of mushroom and garlic and cabbage and parsley. Ohhh...mmmm...

A battering clattering heralded Michelle, gate-crashing with a hostess trolley precariously piled with dessert dishes stained by remains of crème brûlée.

"*Oh là là,* Jessica*! Ma petite marmiteuse*! Ohh, Madame she is angry! '*La Bitche* will clean every *soucoupe*! *La Bitche* will polish every *plateau*!'" Michelle mirthed and mimicked, and was gone.

I paused and mused the menu, discarded amid the debris of those four consummate courses:

Bouillabaisse
Poulet farci aux champignons
Fromage
Crème brûlée

Then excitedly I seized the leftover place cards. They would betray the names of those noisome New Nazis! But wait, these made absolutely no sense! Lithium? Boron? Nitrogen? Fluorine? Sodium? Aluminium? Phosphorus? Chlorine? Oh, if only I'd paid any attention in Miss Slagg's chemistry lessons!

"WHAT you are doing with *les marques-places, imbécile?*"

Yeow! I hadn't heeded the sneaky, stealthy entry of

Madame. I squealed and squirmed and so-near shat myself as she moodily mouthed her ireful interrogative.

All fright and fluster, I replied, "Madame, jer surlemont daysear lay sooveneer!"

From the passageway, a doorbell sang its sonorous sequence of xylophonic notes, a parrot-like "Aark, Aark" joined the grating groaning of a gate and a lovely, lilty, sweetly-sexy, Valley-Welsh voice spoke...

"Hiya, Jessica Jenkins yurr. Sori I'm so lêt, my caa broke down, pain in the aase, it is. Cun I still do anythin yiwssful for yiw, or am I too lêt now? So sori!"

...and inwardly I winced as my inevitable detection threatened and thundered.

Madame's porcine eyes maddened and morphed from murky, muddy brown to angry, pearly black. Her whole body, her whole being, contorted and distorted, as if an extra-terrestrial writhed within her, struggling to keep itself secret. She slowly, silently shut the door with muted, malevolent triumph.

"Ahh, Madame can all see! You are not the waitress of the *bureau de placement*. You are the *espionne anglaise*! *Perruche*!"

"Madame, *NON*!" I protested, stuttering, stammering. "I-I swear! I-I just need the money! That's all!"

"You ave need of the *monnaie* and you wear a *Gigi Giselle*? Pah! Madame is not *stupide*! *Perruche*!"

Sometimes, caught is caught; explanations and excuses elude us. Panicking and palpitating, I let those place cards fall fluttering to the floor, telltale tears inking confession down my mascara-mired cheeks.

"You think Madame is angry, *peut-être?* Ahh, *non*! Madame is kind! Madame is *généreuse*! You will ride my orse! Ohh, *oui*! E is a magic orse! E no can speak, but e make the others for to speak! Ahh, *oui*! You will speak, *ma belle anglaise*! You will tell to me all, after you ave *montée à mon cheval*!"

7

Angelae Ex Machinae

As angsty and angry as I felt for my fate, I could scarcely smother my sniggers when at last Perruche slipped softly into the scullery. Her shoulder-length barley-blonde hair scruffy and straggly, her baby-blue eyes languid and lurid, her broad, beaky nose overhanging her scrunched-up lips and proudly pointy chin, in all she reminded me of a papier-mâché puppet in a junior school Punch and Judy play. In anxious habit, repeatedly she shrugged her shoulders, animating her arms with an argumentative "Aark!" Her garish grass-green dress and scarlet cardigan sealed her parroty, puppety appearance.

"*Perruche, l'Anglaise est pour le cheval.*" Madame motioned, in an 'off-with-her-head' kind of way, causing a seemingly satisfied smile to spread the breadth of that avian face. Then an image fixed in the slideshow of my mind, of a naked woman, wrists tied, astride a wooden apex, grimacing and gaping, her searing, silent torturer slowly, inexorably extorting confession. The Spanish Horse. I'd hit on it by accident, surfing for 'Spanish Horses' before visiting Vienna's famed and fabled Lipizzaner Stallions.

And now that brace of bitches began their pincer attack, each inching imperceptibly either side of that big bad butcher-block table. No *way* would they impale *me* on that terrible, torturous horse! But which one of the two to tackle through? Perruche's lithe eyes implied intercepting instinct; Madame's heavy hands suggested manly-muscular strength. Seconds slipped speedily through my fingers. My heads-or-tails deliberations fell for rushing Perruche, for powering past, for dashing into the blackness of the night. But with an angry, awful "Aark! Aark!" Perruche flung herself at me gridiron style. We scrummed and scrabbled before I broke loose but, with a sickening, sinking sensation I felt Madame's unnaturally harsh hands tighten their gruesome grip around my flailing forearms.

"NO!" I wailed, protesting, panicking. "NO!"

"*Perruche, sa bouche*," commanded Madame, hauling my hands behind my back while, as I gaped and gasped in shock, Perruche pulled from her pocket a mangy, manky, snotty hanky and stuffed it dextrously and determinedly into my mouth. My mind began to spin and swim as if I rode a merry-go-round, my life disintegrating and dissolving around my head, no longer mine to command or comprehend. A rope tightened and tautened my wincing wrists, that grotty, snotty hanky stopped my muffled mouth. Then led away, led away, arm in arm along another bright white corridor all lumps and bumps and grim grey granite casements, to a door, through a door, to a hall of mirrors, a wall of mirrors, then flung frantic to the floor, a pale pine floor, alongside an ancient oaken contraption, varnished black and brown with age – a Spanish Horse! I squealed in awe and anguish.

"For why suffer, *Anglaise*?" reasoned Madame. "Tell to me all. *Beichte macht dich frei*! Hah!"

And without another word, my inquisitors condemned me to an inky blackness, to an impenetrable, deep-space darkness, defying even eyes enriched with choicest carrots. And yet, somehow still I sensed the 'abomination that causes desolation' standing silent sentinel over me, readied to impart its cleaving, crippling interrogation at Madame's perverted pleasure.

And now I began to cry. To cry like I had never cried. To cry like I'd cried the evening my father had died. To grizzle like I'd grizzled as the drops of glue had dripped, dripped, dripped from their nozzle and onto the flight deck of my model HMS *Ark Royal* as Mother, callous and comfortless, had imparted the traumatising, terrifying news. Now, I fell to bawling and boohooing as I remembered my exotic borders of peacock-blue agapanthus, oriole-orange canna and canary-yellow kniphofia; to wailing and waahaaing as I recalled Gwynfor showering his slippers with his pout-pink watering can and Gloria caressing my senses with her cinnamon-scented cakes. Oh, what had been so wrong with deadly dull?

And then a sudden stomach-swell signalled a pyroclastic spurt of sick. Just in time I poked that hanky out from my mouth with my tongue, as the hot torrent of ill-tasting chicken and mushroom and cabbage and parsley and garlic spewed semi-digested through my teeth like an acrid coq au vin. I shivered and shuddered and sobbed with sorrow and shame. Oh, these were no fashionable fair-weather Fascists, these were the real neo-Nazi deal! I'd die here, on that torture horse, blurting a bullied betrayal of Uncle Charles and Lady Godiva, in my sick-stained waitress-wear.

Torpid with terror, my frozen heart within my fearful breast bid me make my final trembling effort: *"Lighten our darkness, we beseech thee, O Lord; and by thy great mercy defend us from all perils and dangers of this night; for the love of thy only Son, our Saviour, Jesus Christ. Amen."*

I never knew how long I lay in dooming darkness, how long awake, how long asleep, surreal schemes of escape intertwining inexorably with doleful, dirgeful death knells, but when at length bright white light scalded at my tight-shut eyes, I dreamed myself ascended into Heaven, my expectations exalted by an angelic apparition before me – golden hair, sapphire eyes, softly, sweetly, smiling... Perruche!

My incredulity increased as Perruche gently pressed her forefinger to her seemingly kindly lips as if to hush me, before gesturing and gesticulating her intentions: Me... You... Untie! A ballet barre extended the length of the mirrored wall and Perruche next mimed and motioned, backing onto the barre with her instructions: You... Me... Tie! Lastly, to drain any dregs of doubt, Perruche concluded by pointing to me, then to the door, finally frenziedly flapping her arms as if to say, "Fly! Fly! Fly!"

"Perruche! You mean to set me free!" I soliloquised, forcing myself to my feet in rhetorical rejoicing. An emphatic euphoria thrilled through me, as when a festering flu bug lifts at last and miraculously the faculties of life and love and hope and heart and invention and inspiration come flooding back.

My emancipatrix nodded, knowingly, glinting tears brightening her orb-like eyes.

Momentarily, the significance of her soft nod was lost. Then the rosy glow of morning inched above the windowsill of my mind, like sunshine spilling across the tufts and tussocks of dew-drenched dawn.

"Perruche! You understand English!"

"Angh! Angh!" attempted Perruche, with torrents of tears running in rivulets, streaking her cheeks, her hands frantically fumbling at my knotted wrists. In dextrous seconds she had set me free.

"Oh, my poor Perruche!" I consoled, cuddling and caressing. "Who *are* you? Who *are* you?"

"Angh! Angh!" braved my beaky, birdy ally.

Oh, I stung with shame, to enslave her to that ballet barre!

"I'll be back, I promise, to set *you* free!" I pledged and pitied. "I'll come back with the Royal Marines!"

And at length, as if delving the depths of an inky, peaty pool, I grasped past the deceiving dappling of that cartoonish, clownish caricature, and held in both hands the fear-struck, tear-struck, genuine girl.

Time to go! Unthinkingly, unhesitatingly, I scampered past that horrid horse to the door just ajar, then peeked out, sneaked out, into the brilliant white cloister-like corridor heavy with hewn stones, then pell-mell to the yukky-yellow door of the scruffy scullery, its crockery and cutlery sparkling resplendent, its sinks stinking stagnant with murky foody water. There lay the place cards, fallen to the floor. Hurriedly I scooped them up and stashed them between my boobs before braving the door that led… OMG, I wasn't sure where! Oh, what to do! If I fucked up, I'd find myself astride that harrowing horse, agonising and anguishing until I'd blurted and spurted every damning detail of MI69.

Daring a sneak peek through the inch-open door, my nose savoured the sweetness of mild night air, fragrant in its Elysian antithesis to the noxious pongs of brackish bouillabaisse and chomped-on champignons. Somewhere, close by, a window or a door left open enticed my escape! I had no option but to gamble on my mad dash for freedom. If I lingered or loitered longer I'd be caught for sure.

Sneaking slowly, silently from my drudgery scullery, I thrilled to find myself five feet from a doorway into darkness. Add twenty yards across the well-remembered stark yard of concrete and chippings to a sodium streetlamp standing sentinel over my archway into liberty… Would it, could it, be this easy?

I tiptoed through the welcoming doorway to be instantly immersed in a flood of phosphorescent light. The entire edifice was illuminated. Shocked and stilled I froze in fright like a bunny in the beams as Madame, poised beside the Brandenburg 800, pointed penetratingly, accusatively, scowling and shouting angrily, "*La bitche anglaise! Elle s'est échappée!*"

Her ugly accomplice, a shaven-skulled brute-faced bruiser, pulled a pistol and aimed. Instinctively I clenched my eyes tight in expectation of indescribable agonies as a shot rang and ricocheted around.

I did not feel the bullet hit me. Instead, stunned, I staggered backwards, falling forwards onto my knees, clutching and grasping at my stomach, and wincing and wailing and writhing and weeping.

Unexpectedly, a comforting, caressing call cut the thick night air. "For fuck's sake, Louise! What the bloody hell are you playing at?"

Tiggi's voice? Oh, dazed delirium! Surely my waning, draining life was ebbing to extremity!

"Oh, Tigg!" I gasped. "Is it really you? Are you really there? Oh, help me, please, Tiggi, I've been shot!"

"No, you haven't, you stupid arse! I shot the thug! His brains spattered the Fat Cow's face and she's fainted! RUN! Come ON!"

What? Not shot? In wide-eyed wonder I heaved relieved as ambrosian elixir enthused and exalted me, daring me and driving me to a bolt-from-the-block sprint-start. Tiggi leaped from the wall in black balaclava, black bodysuit and black boots, brandishing in both hands the biggest, baddest gunmetal grey pistol I'd ever shuddered to see. Together we fled past the half-headed corpse messed with brains and blood, then across the tangerine beams of lamplight, and hurtled and hurled ourselves over the low stone wall into Les Jardins des Mémoires.

8

All She Said

A benign night greeted us. A magnificent moon, radiant and luminous, cast shadows, gaunt and gnarled, from the spindly, spiny shrubs of Les Jardins des Mémoires, their herbaceous fragrances heavy on the mild night air. The softly sounding seas shone silver on black, while the *tink-tink-tink* from the rigging of the bobbing boats soothed hushed Sainte-Modeste into her dreamy sleep. A gratuitous, gratified "Oh! Oh! Oh!" of penetrated pleasure momentarily broke the sweet stillness, then was silent.

"We're as good as safe," assured Tiggi, smiling. "The Bald Thug and the Fat Cow were the last to leave. When the Fat Cow comes round, the last thing on *her* mind will be scouring the streets for *us*."

"I hope to heaven you're right," I puffed and panted. "I couldn't run another step. I'm fucked."

"We'll lie low overnight in Dave Lanchbury's apartment. I'll put an 'Extricate' into HQ from there."

Dave's name on Tiggi's lips drew a titillating thrill to my dart-struck heart.

"Do you *know* Dave Lanchbury?"

"*Know* him? He's worked for MI69 these past five years."

"SHIT!" I squeaked. Ohh, had I been *had*! Dave had known who I was all along! Ohh, the *SOD*!

"Something wrong?" wheedled Tiggi, with a wry smirk.

"No, nothing," I demurred. "I might just have behaved a little differently towards him, had I known."

"Don't worry," tittered Tiggi. "I'm *sure* he won't have taken you the wrong way."

Ohh! She *knew*! She KNEW! Inwardly I cringed, outwardly I craved the countenance of a countess.

Tiggi snaked her mamba-like arm through mine. "This way," she hissed, "down through Neuveville."

Neuveville comprised two cliff-clinging, serpentine streets meandering beyond the bastions and bulwarks of the tumbledown Louis-Quatorze walls of Sainte-Modeste, testimony to the tenacity of the seventeenth-century townsfolk, built by them on the only fragments of terra firma between the opulent orchards of Le Monastère and the rock-tossed seas beneath. Architects divined decades of development in the corbels and casements of those twisting, turning, up-and-down streets, every dwelling added ad hoc as each artisan or mariner or fisherman or merchant had needed. Twice had I ventured with touristy curiosity into those higgledy-piggledy alleyways only to be spewed, lost, time after time into the fountained Place des Voiliers. Tiggi, however, was as sure-footed as a Sherpa amid the crags and crannies of Neuveville. Within minutes, the welcoming reds and yellows and greens and blues illuminating the Old Harbour lent their fleeting paints to our fleeing figures.

As we neared Dave's apartment, a staggering Joanne cackled incredulously at our kinky costumes as drunkenly she slip-slid her clumsy key into her own latch-lock, chortling, "I'm not even gonna ask!"

"Oh, wouldn't you *love* to *know*!" teased Tiggi, as we sneaked sleazily through Dave's door.

The flat felt thick with darkness. Nonetheless, Tiggi's shaded silhouette stood against the greyness as she held my hands and whispered wantonly, winningly, "So, Louise, how about a lovely big kiss for the girl who's just saved your life?"

I felt totally torn in two, plagued by pheromones in cosmic combat around and about me.

"Oh, Tigg!" I half-enthused, half-excused. "I'm so grateful, so grateful, but – oh, I don't *know*!"

"*What?*" flipped Tiggi. "You don't *know*?"

"It's just – Dave and I got on so well, and…"

"UGH!" uttered Tiggi, half-screaming, half-squealing. "You BITCH!" And I felt the flat of her hand smack stinging into my right cheek. Then, "You BITCH!" as her other smashed sobering into my left.

Slapped and stunned beyond stuttering a syllable in self-defence, I snivelled, sobbing and smarting.

"You self-centred back-sliding *BITCH*, Louise Fawley! What have I got to do to stop you hankering after *MEN*? Don't you realise that if your so-called Uncle Charles doesn't cover my arse I'll spend the next twenty years in *PRISON* for what I've just done! I had no *RIGHT* to kill that fucking Ugly Thug! I'm on suspension, under investigation, thanks to Charmian frigging Mudher! If they lock me up they're going to throw away the bloody key! And all you can whinge and whine is, 'Dave and I got on so well'. OHH! I thought *WE* got on pretty well at Vetchley, you selfish cow, or maybe that all slipped your mind?"

"But, Tigg," I whinged, all snotty and sniffy, "didn't Uncle Charles send you?" I felt giddily bewildered.

Tiggi's black shadow glided through the gloom. A switch flicked, and Dave's wholesome home instantly illuminated. Her bewitching behind strutted into the hallowed haven of Dave's bedroom. Seconds later she returned. Her black balaclava was absent now, and her amber-auburn mane sprang angrily about her red-hot face, smeared with tears, softened only by her soothing, chestnut eyes.

Tiggi carried a pink and purple plastic treasure chest, of a sort sold to serve as a toy-box, then set it down on the coffee table. With another wry, dry smile, she lifted the lid, then flung like fireworks in ones and twos and threes in every direction knickers, panties, tangas, shorties, G-strings, lacies, thongs, skimpies, in pink, scarlet, emerald, sapphire, ivory, lilac, purple, cream. To each purloined pair was tied a tiny brown-paper label. I grabbed one: 'Agnieszka 17.8.17'; I snatched another: 'Sofia 24.12.15'; I clutched a third: 'Elena 28.4.18'; I plucked a fourth: 'Laura 14.2.16'. And throughout the whole humiliating spectacular Tiggi sardonically catalogued the capitulated: "There's a Justine… oh, we've got a Liesel…hey, another Rhiannon…ooh, a Chantal this time…" And there – there on the fluffy faux-fur hearth rug – there lay my scruffy, scuzzy sky-blue Shane & Sheila skimpies.

"So, you *still* suppose you've got something special with Dave?" Tiggi mocked sarcastically.

As an antelope, exhausted by her bouncing, bounding efforts to escape, beaten, bends to the inevitable incisors, so I, softly, sobbingly, submissively, sweetly surrendered to my lioness lover-girl.

"Now, let's try this a second time. How about a lovely big kiss for the girl who's just saved your life?"

"Oh *yes*, Tigg!" I begged, deliciously defeated and delightfully disillusioned. "*Now*, Tigg! *Please*, Tigg!"

Tiggi puckered her luscious, luxurious, glistening lips, cradled my cheeks between her gentle palms, then pressed her proudly pouting kiss against mine. My head spun and swam as our tongues tickled and entwined, tentatively, tenderly, but shockingly, suddenly Tiggi reeled and recoiled in distaste and disgust.

"UGH! You've been SICK! Oh, for fuck's sake, Louise! Go and wash your mouth out and get to bed!"

Unexpectedly, my mind flashed back to that hateful, hurtful horse, to the ballet barre and the pale pine floor.

Then inexplicably, my chest leadened, my throat dried and tightened, my breathing grew lengthy and laboured, until inhalation and exhalation demanded my every effort. My frightened eyes sought succour from the mustard walls, the chocolate sofas, the burgundy cushions…

"Oh, Tiggi!" I breathed, between heaving, halting gasps. "Please help me! I think I'm…think I'm…"

Tiggi morphed in moments from predator to protector. Caringly, caressingly, again she chaperoned my shaking hands within her genteel grasp, her glistening eyes all looking and loving and longing.

"Louise, relax. You're having a panic attack, that's all. Breathe normally. That's it…in…out…in…out…"

My rabid respiration subsided slowly to nearly normal. Still, I scarcely dared move for fright.

"Heaven Almighty, Louise! What *happened* to you in there? You really do need to tell me!"

"Oh, Tigg! You *did* save my life! How on *earth* did you know where to rescue me?"

Tiggi slumped and sprawled into a sofa. I snuggled secure and demure alongside.

"When Charmian suspended me, I was raging with hate and hurt. I drove home dazed and demented, oblivious to everything but my own red-hot tears. Charmian had decided that I'd acted improperly by permitting myself to become infatuated with you, that I'd abused my position as mentor by trying to get close to you. Pah. I've got *nothing* to be ashamed of. But what destroyed me came next day when she locked me out of Scrapbook and I couldn't check that you were safe. The cow! It was *my* idea to use Scrapbook for operational communication in the first place. With all those snapshots and snippets bouncing through the ether, it's the perfect camouflage for Godiva's little secret messages.

"Well, fuck MI69, I thought. There was nothing to prevent me journeying down to Sainte-Modeste and holidaying there myself. Only I was thick enough to think that you'd be bored out of your brain with *Wines of the World* and moonstruck to see me. That was until yesterday evening, when I arrived at Hôtel Louis-Philippe to be told that you hadn't been seen since Saturday, but the nudge-nudge wink-wink was that you had gone away for a few days with Monsieur Lanchbury. Ohh! I felt insulted and outraged and humiliated and betrayed and violated! To picture you relishing your double-dogging by that lecherous Lothario! Ugh! And I'd stupidly shafted my entire career *because* of you!

"I wandered through Les Jardins des Mémoires intending to soak up the setting sun and contemplate the rest of my life. I'd scarcely got to the top when I heard a crazy commotion from the road and, in a nasty raspy bark, '*Vite! Vite!* Already you are in *retard*!' and, in a pleading, panicking squeal, 'Madame! Jer vooz on pree! Jer ner swee paa een serverze!' YOUR voice! Hurriedly I hobbled all high heels and handbag to help you, but by the time I'd reached the roadside, the Place de Leny was empty.

"Well, I was scarcely clothed for combat – I was scarcely clothed at all – so I scampered back to my Hôtel Impérial as speedily as my heels would clatter. Even so it was a good hour later that, clad in black with pistol primed, I scrambled up the crumbly villa wall to find a place to hide, watching and waiting.

"Two waitresses scurried out and hurried off. One was Welsh. 'She can't just've vanished,' she lilted. The other was French. 'We owe to tell to the police,' she urged. I *knew* they were talking of you. Then guests started departing in twos and threes as car after car convoyed to collect them. Five left together in a black Bayern B6. At last, only the Bald Thug and the Fat Cow were left, sharing hushed conspiratorial whispers. Until out you bounced in all your glory like the fairy on the Christmas tree."

"Michelle and Jessica – they were fearful for my safety!" I marvelled. Their concerned comradeship felt miraculous following the noxious nastiness of Madame. "Of course! I remember now! They'd finished the washing up, but they hadn't drained the sink! They must've left as soon as they'd dared!"

"And now, ma chérie, we really *do* need to get some sleep. You go and clean yourself up, and I'll put in our SOS to HQ. It's about the only thing I'm still allowed to do. Oh, Charmian's going to shaft my arse for this!"

In Dave's bathroom, I found some gangrene green minty mouthwash, so stood gargling and gurgling until the tainted taste of chickeny sick had tingled refreshingly from my mouth. In Sarah's bedroom, I found some red-nosed reindeer patterned pyjamas, so gratefully changed, ridding myself finally of those dig-in thigh-highs and that agonising waistband. Those kooky chemical element place cards fluttered to the floor once more. This time, I plucked them up and stuffed them in my pyjamas pocket.

Yawning with sleepiness, yearning for slumbers, suddenly that sense of minxing mirthful mischief, which had so badly blotted my schoolgirl jotter, bubbled up inside me, daring me to dunk Dave's toothbrush down and around the sick-stained sink. Hah! I sniggered to think of him wondering at his strange-tasting toothpaste. As I stumbled bedward, I snatched my sky-blue Shane & Sheila skimpies from his hearthrug. No way was he making a safari trophy of those! I fumbled at their little brown-paper label, expecting to read a cataloguing name and date. Instead, I stood shocked into stillness to see scrawled simply, 'The One'.

9

Orangette

A scarcely snatched sleep and a frantic, frenetic flurry of sartorial adornment later, Tiggi Trebarwith and Louise Fawley strode silkily arm in arm through the somnolent salon de café of the haughty Hôtel Napoléon. Ooh, how deliciously, how mouth-wateringly our two names inextricably intertwined in the velvet valentine chocolate-box of my wild mind! Louise and Tiggi, Tiggi and Louise… Mentally I masticated, masturbated, on that honeyed couplet, on its togetherness, its foreverness…ohh!

At Tiggi's insistence, we'd each tweaked our style of attire as far as Sarah's ransacked racks of rags would allow. Tiggi had snatched a Breton top in navy and white, and teamed with navy denim jeggings and bright white plimsolls, she oozed nautical naughtiness. I'd swiped a floaty, flouncy tangerine blouse, some flirty, flaunty bad-in-black leggings, and black daps. To accessorise, we'd each stolen a Riley headscarf and handbag set, cream for Tiggi, orange for me. Our visages positively plastered with pale skin perfector, our trouty lips and lazy eyelids languid under their garish, gaudy purple maquillage. No one would ever have guessed that we were two gay girls giving the slip to a bunch of neo-Nazi nasties.

Nonetheless, I rued and regretted that we couldn't simply slip into my mile-munching Montvecchio Tarantella to ease our escape through heaven-sent, heavily scented Provence.

"Louise, we've got to get a table at the far end, with views around the Marina. That's what Charmian said."

"Oh, Tiggi! What on *earth* made you take the train all the way down to the south of France?"

"I could scarcely smuggle *this* beauty aboard an aeroplane," tittered Tiggi, patting her pistol-packed handbag. "It's a Stellenbosch 997 with dum-dum bullets, completely contrary to every convention of course. Oh, the pain in the arse it gave me just sneaking it out of the United States! In the end I was forced to ship Piran a crateful of second-hand tractor spares, and hide it in the middle of those."

"Hm. The pain in the arse it gave *you* was nothing to the pain in the *head* it gave that guy last night."

"I've never killed anyone before," pondered Tiggi. "I feel I should feel something, but I fear I don't feel anything.

Just a great big anti-climax. Like the morning after I lost my virginity. Like, was that *IT*?"

After pawing and purring our catwalk way to the remotest tables, we positioned our posteriors on those harsh, hard, wooden-slatted seats, with every semblance of elegance we could counterfeit.

"You know what I'd love to eat right now, Tigg? A cream tea: sultana scones, clotted cream, strawberry jam and a pot of Earl Grey. I'm absolutely ravenous!"

"I hardly think you're going to find sultana scones down here on the Côte d'Azur. You'll have to manage the best you can with a café noir and a croissant."

"Ha. Who needs sultana scones, when I can lick my jam and cream from your beautiful bare behind?"

"Ugh, you're *disgusting*! Just remember I'm a Cornish girl and make sure you spread your jam on first."

"Like it matters. Do you still have those crazy place cards?"

"In my bag. Nitrogen, Lithium, Sodium, Chlorine, Phosphorus, Fluorine…I can't make head or tail."

"I'm *sure* there were more."

"Fluorine – isn't that the one that whizzes and fizzes around in a big glass bowl full of water?"

"I think so…by the name. And I'm pretty sure sodium turns limewater milky."

New Harbour originated before the Great War, in the dying decades of earnest commerce at Sainte-Modeste. Nowadays, the surviving vestiges of industrial heritage amounted to an occasional giant iron mooring-post embedded in the glistening-granite blocks comprising the harbourside. The fishing fleet had vanished with the fish; the guano trade had dried up with the guano. Now, only the clean white cabin cruisers bobbing like seagulls at their pontoon moorings sardined the Marina; only the glass-and-chrome of artfully arrayed apartments afforded a backdrop, like concrete building blocks.

My mind mesmerised to the hypnotic, narcotic, to and fro of the gently restless murky, mucky waters, their subtly shifting palette of reflected dabs taking shimmering shape as prows and sterns, masts and rails, floats and ropes, deckhouses and gunwales. In the lap-lap shallows, a troupe of terns idled their tranquil time, as a brace of the serenest swans glided gracefully by in perfect pas-de-deux.

"*Voilà, Mademoiselles! Les trois Orangettes!*"

The waiter, a swarthy, stubbly Spaniard with cheery, chestnut eyes and manly, moustachioed grin cradled carefully three tiny trays in opulent oranges and brilliant blues, each bearing a bottle of chilled Orangette, a glass tumbler, a crisp white napkin and sweet sugared biscuits, all in high colonial style.

"*Pour la mademoiselle…et pour la mademoiselle…et pour le monsieur… Bon appétit!*"

Pour le monsieur? In consternation, Tiggi and I eyed each other, dreading, panicking, hoping for help. Tiggi slid her hand inside her Riley bag for her saviour Stellenbosch. I clenched myself in sheer fear.

Alfonso – as badged – ambled away, flicking at flies with his tea towel. And neither of us noticed a guy gently, subtly, silently seating himself beside us, behind his greying goatee beard and fading fawn suit.

It was Richard de Leny.

10

Still Small Voice

"In Moscow," narrated de Leny drily, "it is already a quarter to three."

"Whereas in Tokyo," rejoined Tiggi, already completely composed, "it is still only half past one."

"And in New York…"

"…it is just about five past five."

"Richard de Leny."

"Tiggi Trebarwith."

They shared a heartfelt handshake. My fears fled. Instead, instantly I felt marginalised and miffed.

"*Excuse* me? Feeling a little left out here. Will one of you kindly explain?"

"Louise," de Leny greeted, "it's lovely to see you."

"You too," I scraped from somewhere.

"In answer to your question, Louise, your Uncle Charles has recruited me too."

"But…"

"Surely I'm mixed up in La Ligne? Well, so I am."

"I'm confused," I complained.

"We're both confused," confirmed Tiggi.

At leisure, de Leny softly, slowly poured his refreshing, revitalising Orangette which, bubbling and brimming with energetic effervescence, enlivened us all with its orangey-lemony fragrance.

"I am authorised to explain myself, girls, should you wish."

"Oh, please *do*!" we enthused in unison.

"OK. Some twelve months ago, I was quite surprised to receive an approach from my distant relation, Armand Lebrun. You may recall, Louise, that my great-aunt Marianne, alas no longer with us, married in 1946 Jean-Claude Lebrun, a captain in the Belgian army, following his return from a German prisoner-of-war camp. The same year, the couple adopted Georges, the boy whom Marianne had found wandering Longueville during the chaos of May 1940, and had cared for throughout the war."

"Oh, *yes*! I remember Georges' sorry story. His parents – whoever they were – never showed up."

"Quite. Well, Armand is the son of Georges. He is an accountant by profession and is finance director of Merde SA, one of the largest manufacturers of bathroom furniture in Europe. Anyway, in the letter that he sent, Armand announced that he was launching La Ligne – a sort of lifeline, I suppose – as a means of assisting families of refugees in settling themselves into new lives within the European Union. His vision was a one-stop shop – La Ligne would effectively recruit and relocate professional people from their war-shattered homelands and transplant them into paradise lifestyles in the West. It would show, he persuaded me, that the Old Nobility of France was equal to assuming a leading role in assuaging some of the ugliest humanitarian disasters of our times."

"I scarcely see how facilitating a brain drain of the educated and enlightened from any nation is likely to be of benefit," preached Tiggi, a tad pompously and priggishly, I felt.

"I was sceptical myself, Miss Trebarwith," admitted de Leny. "But so little seemed to be happening to help. A ceaseless stream of refugees seemingly sleepwalking from one side of Europe to the other." De Leny's nostrils dilated, subtly, slightly. Otherwise, not the faintest flicker of feeling fell from his face.

"So, disregarding the fact that Armand Lebrun is not, of course, of the Old Nobility of France, at length Léonard, Lionel and I all agreed to support his La Ligne. We each stumped up our one million euros."

"Fucking hell!" I exclaimed. "You gave him three million euros?"

"You'll think us silly, Louise, I'm sure. But his impeccable credentials, the painstaking professionalism with which he delivered his dossier, led all three of us to think La Ligne a sincere, serious, scheme."

"But...it wasn't?"

"Three months ago, following newswire after newswire each extolling in ever more unconvincing tones the progress of La Ligne, we were finally relieved to receive a brochure featuring Yusuf al-Hakim, a Syrian doctor settled successfully with his family in Bad Bieden, a tiny town in north-western Hesse. A heart-warming letter of gratitude from Yusuf was edged with pictures of the Family al-Hakim relishing their new lives – his wife baking pastries, their children playing on swings and slides, that sort of thing."

"Sounds like a happy ending."

"Well. You'll understand it when I tell you, Louise, that my wife's acute arthritis has now grown so debilitating as to preclude our ever venturing on holiday. Even going shopping has become an impossible ordeal for her. And how Dilys adored her trips abroad! So nowadays, if ever I'm heading off on a business trip, Dilys insists I spin it out by a day or two, to find time for some solo sightseeing."

"That's Dilys. Always thoughtful."

"Thank you. Well, four weeks ago I was in Frankfurt, gathering backing for our new joint venture with the Sultan of Lakash. My meetings went splendidly well, leaving me feeling so buoyed that I resolved to pay a surprise call on the Family al-Hakim, only fifty minutes' drive to the north. All I could recall was their address, 16 Richard-Wagner-Strasse, but I felt assured of finding them in such a small town."

"And did you?"

"Louise, Bad Bieden doesn't even have a Richard-Wagner-Strasse."

My lips involuntarily parted as, stunned stupefied, I struggled with what de Leny's news might mean.

"Then, several nights later when, safely home, I was still deliberating what I ought to do and whom I ought to tell, my offices at Melusine Plastics were burgled. Well, I say burgled. Nothing was actually stolen."

A smirk spread the breadth of Tiggi's purple-pouting lips. I longed to kick her shin, but didn't dare.

"And, a few days following my statement to Detective Sergeant Joanne Oates, your Commander Chumleigh presented himself at Melusine Plastics, declaring his intense interest in the matter."

I dreaded the direction this discourse was tending. I recalled de Leny's stinging teasing all too painfully.

"I couldn't help feeling that there was something somewhat familiar in the burglar's trail of destructive incompetence. And I couldn't help wondering just how many people had known of my broken window. But almost the only clue Stuart could offer was that the burglarette was blessed with a big bottom."

Tiggi's cackling laughter burst like a breached dam and de Leny sniggered like a sizzling sausage.

"Oh, ha bloody ha, the pair of you! Oh, you're so flipping funny! Oh, *please* stop laughing, I'll cry! Oh, this is so *humiliating*! Tiggi, tell him about the place cards! I found a clue, the place cards! Oh, *please*!"

"Haa…! Yes…! Haa…! Yes, the place cards! Hee! Here…Mr de Leny…the place cards! Hee!"

My former boss browsed through those unfathomable cards one by one. It seemed so strange to reminisce upon the countless times I had stood silently at his side as he had patiently, ploddingly perused some inscrutable set of monthly management figures for positive pointers to performance.

"Louise, if I understand your report to Miss Trebarwith correctly, Armand Lebrun and his – I scarcely can strain myself to say it – New Nazis…held a full three-course dinner in the *grande salle à manger*?"

"Yeah. Turd Soup, some sort of Chicken Kiev, and Cream Broolays."

"Then I believe we may safely say that there were eighteen of them."

"Eighteen?" quizzed Tiggi. "How can you be so sure?"

"I'd have guessed at about eighteen," I chipped, "from the amount of dirty dishes."

"Quite so. These…Lithium, Nitrogen, Fluorine, Sodium, Phosphorus, Chlorine…are respectively the third, seventh, ninth, eleventh, fifteenth and seventeenth elements in the Periodic Table. I'd wager that originally you had place cards for Boron and Aluminium too?"

"Boron, definitely."

"Then picture a large dining table. Agents Hydrogen and Helium sit at either end – Armand and his sister Adolphine, I'd conjecture, with Agents Lithium, Boron, Nitrogen, Fluorine, Sodium, Aluminium, Phosphorus, and

Chlorine, along one side, and Agents Beryllium, Carbon, Oxygen, Neon, Magnesium, Silicon, Sulphur, and Argon, along the other."

"That's brilliant!" exuded Tiggi.

"Dare I say," ventured de Leny, "*elementary*?"

"Oh, *please*!" I moaned. "Your jokes haven't improved."

"Add to this the fact that, when fully extended, the dining table in the *grande salle à manger* seats eighteen, and I'd suggest it's as good as certain."

"But why Nazis?" searched Tiggi. "I mean, Armand and Adolphine don't exactly have anything in common with the disillusioned and dispossessed of the depression-ridden 1930s."

"I've pondered on that," mused de Leny. "My great-aunt Nicole, who lived at Longueville throughout the war, always maintained that Georges was an odd boy. You see, my great-grandfather was elderly and sickly, and my great-uncle played the aristocratic buffoon to conceal his part in the Résistance, so the only positive male role models young Georges saw were the dashing, charming Luftwaffe fighter pilots, quartered on the château. His childhood dream became that when he grew up, he would learn to fly a Messerschmitt, take to the skies against the RAF, and win the war for the Reich. When, instead, the Americans liberated the château, he first bawled the old place down, then didn't speak for weeks."

"So, you think he nurtured an infatuation with Nazism and transmitted it to his children?"

"An infatuation you might call it, Miss Trebarwith. I'm

sure I'd choose an uglier word myself."

De Leny sipped subtly at his Orangette, before resuming. "You see, Miss Trebarwith, history moulds and sculpts us, and we, in our turn, sculpt and mould history. Take the great guns of Sainte-Modeste. They were, in fact, French guns, taken from the old battleship *Hué*, and manned by Frenchmen until weeks before the end of the war. When the gunners deserted to join the advancing Free French, it was a clumsy coincidence that amid the chaotic collapse, a unit of Wehrmacht artillerymen retreated upon Sainte-Modeste. And yet, it's their surrender to the local Résistance that's brilliantly immortalised in bronze, and the great French guns are remembered as German guns. Indeed, the turrets and magazines of the *Hué* still exist, buried beneath Les Jardins."

Unexpectedly, de Leny's countenance grew grim and grey like granite, as speedily as a wind-whipped cloud shifts sunny into shady.

"Ladies, I very much fear that the couple just arrived wouldn't long countenance our discourse on historiography. Don't look. Louise, Tiggi, we'll rise quietly, then stroll slowly together through that gate into Rue des Plongeurs where, so I'm reliably informed, Agent Daniel Smith will be waiting with a sunset-orange Voortrekker 4x4 to speed us to our privately chartered Kent 250 jet at Aéroport Nice."

I dared a darting glance starboard, and shuddered scared to mark that horrid hairy harridan Madame, her black bob dirty-lank, her evil eyes piggy-deep, a thuggishly ugly brutish bruiser by her side.

Fourth Movement

Bonquonne

1

At Hexhurst Gardens

Sergeant O'Malley wearily wiped the greasy grime from beneath his war-worn but ever-twinkling eyes, then yanked out the circular steel pin with his incisors. Gripping and kissing his grenade, whispering a prayer into the heat-baked, hard-beaten ground, he propped himself as high as he dared with his left, while catapulting his grenade towards the Wehrmacht machine-gun nest with his right. "That's for O'Rourke and O'Reilly!" he bellowed, vengefully, as squeals of "Achtung! Granate!" seared his ears.

Of course, all we could see and hear were Helen's young sons roughing-and-tumbling across the painstakingly pampered lawns of Hexhurst Gardens Tea Rooms, exchanging bursts of *da-da-da-da-da* from their yellow-and-purple toy assault rifles, shuttlecocking deadly grenades ingeniously improvised from drunk-up Fruit Beaut bottles, writhing and wriggling around their imaginary brotherly battlefield.

Helen was without doubt the most magnificently mumsie of my few true friends. In sky-blue sweater, jet-black jeggings, and muck-marked olive-green wellies she relaxed recumbent, exuding calm contentment. Nowadays, no vanities evoked the slightest spark in her. No Achilles, no Aeneas, could distract her devotion to those two brothers, suckled wolf-like, as if the Gaius and Lucius of their land.

The low-lying, last-of-summer sun spread its sickly embers over all. The stunning clipped hibiscus, the shocking pink agapanthus, the majestic centenarian cedars, the mesmeric gentle grasses, all bathed in glorious oranges and crimsons, presaging the decadent autumnal anarchies of yellows and browns.

"It beats me, Helen. Put me in a room with a hundred men, there might be one I *wouldn't* fancy. Put me in a room with a hundred women, there might be one I *would* fancy. Put me in a room with Tiggi Trebarwith, I'll be gushing like Niagara Falls."

"It isn't so very strange. You're probably a '1' or a '2' on the Kinsey Scale."

"The *what*? The *Kinsey Scale*? Oh, sometimes I *hate* Planet Earth! Here I am, seeking to sound out my deepest, my most intimate feelings, and you're trying to tell me that someone up at Cambridge has already got them plotted out on a graph!"

"It wasn't Cambridge. It was Indiana. And it doesn't hold any correlation. It's a simple integer scale."

"Well, trust you to know all about it, Super Swot. You never ever got the cane, even."

"Louise, *most* girls at St Lucy's never received the cane. I'd say you and Miranda Midgeworthy had more between you than the whole of the rest of the school put together. You were both so *naughty*."

"*Me*, naughty? Pah! The teachers all picked on me because I was almost an orphan."

"*You* weren't naughty? What about our first cookery class at the start of the fourth form? Miss Prigg had brought a beautiful big bowlful of greengages to teach us how to make tart, and you began flicking them around the kitchen classroom, pretending you were picking great green bogeys from your nose!"

"I *never*! It's a *fib*! It's a *fib*! Oh *shit*, I *DID*, didn't I? Doh! What a horrid little bitch I must've been!"

"But then, you were capable of amazing creativity too. Remember that poem you wrote for the school magazine? We'd been studying the American Civil War for History, and The Book of Revelation for Religious Studies, and you came up with 'Pickett's Yell'. Its first verse is etched in my memory:

They say, that on that Judgement Day
Then Pickett's Men shall rise again

And weeping, hug their brothers black
And standing with them, back to back
Confront the Cloven Foe.

Louise, it was inspired. I never understood why you wouldn't or couldn't keep up the good work."

I sighed, reflecting, retreating. "I never understood it either. After my father passed away, I felt infected by this insatiable need for naughtiness. Pain became…strangely comforting."

My gaze dreamed melancholically away across the neatly green lawn to a woodpigeon with plumpish, pinkish tummy and battleship-grey back surrounded by sparrows in harlequin browns all chirping and chomping and gorging on gorgeous cake crumbs, the pigeon like a cumbersome aircraft carrier escorted by welcoming, well-wishing trawlers and tugboats all hooting and tooting their hellos.

Helen smiled with whimsical faraway yesterday eyes. "Do you remember that funny little nun who used to call from the convent to give us singing lessons?"

"Oh, Sister Walburga! She was *charming*! She was *sweet*!"

"And those musty old songbooks?"

"And the *songs*!"

A solitary sparrow, pluckier than her playmates, hopped and halted within inches of Helen, who held out a hand proffering cake-treat, but the sparrow fluttered fearful into the dark depths of an ivy bush.

Intuitively, instinctively, spontaneously, smilingly, we spurted into song:

My spar-row's flown a-way
A-nd will no more come to me
I've broke a glass to-o-da-a-a-a-ay
I've broke a glass to-o-da-a-a-a-ay
The price will quite un-do-o-o-o-o me
Gos-sip Joan!

"Yayy! Yayy!" cheered an ever-eager friendly family of American tourists. "Hooray for Gossip Joan!" And away they strode, all grins and goodwill and cameras and chinos and chuckles and chatter.

At which, the woodpigeon shot off like a sea-to-air missile, his grey shape die-straight acutely angled.

"You know, Louise, you should marry. What you need is someone to straighten you out."

"I don't *need* straightening out. I'm not a penis."

"Hugo is still sweet on you."

"Oh, *please*! There would be thirty-two in that marriage! Me and Hugo and a herd of Gloucester Spots! I mean, I know he's your little brother and all, *but still!*"

"Oh, *Louise*! He isn't as pig-mad as he *was*. And anyway, they're Oxford Sandy-and-Blacks."

My mind mesmerised, lost amid the amber-basked lawns and borders of ambient late afternoon. Maybe, I meditated, this sunset should mark farewell to my frittered, fickle younger years. Perhaps I could, should, still seek a housewarming husband, with delectable, devotional boy-and-girl bundle.

"Why not let me hold a dinner party? You and Hugo,

Peter and I? Oh, *do* say yes, Louise!"

But before I dared 'yea' or 'nay', a sturdy, stalwart shadow slowly spread its pall across our picnic patch; hair on head, suited shoulders, undulating tummy, umbrella in hand... Then, the shadow spoke.

"Well, well, well! Your maiden voyage into espionage has proven quite the sensation!"

"Uncle Charles!" I exulted, ecstatic, leaping from my grassy carpet, clinging to that loveable, huggable navy blue pinstripe persona, drinking deep of his nostalgic commingling of spicy-scented aftershave and lime-laced hair-cream. "Oh, I'm so happy, so happy, to see you again!"

"Mrs Gisburne, I'm in danger of becoming crushed to death by your old school chum!"

"Louise, for goodness' sake! Put him down! Commander Chumleigh, you're very welcome to join our little picnic. We've pork sausages, pork pie, exquisite chutney, all our own. Oh, and fruitcake!"

"You two *know* each other?" I queried, suffering dizzying déjà vu.

"Louise, whom *don't* I know among the inhabitants of this scepter'd isle of ours? Mrs Helen Gisburne has proven invaluable to MI69 frequently. She is our eyes and ears within New Forest society."

We sprawled around our dwindling repast, Uncle Charles helping himself to a flute of champagne and a generous, gorgeous slice of sweetest fruit cake. I dipped my second sausage deep into the tasty, tangy chutney. Helen nibbled at jelly-juicy pork pie pastry, saving the savoury for her battling boys.

"Louise, your recognising that those chemical element place cards had significance was truly a breakthrough moment – an instance of the quintessence of Project Godiva. We had, of course, noted a hieroglyphic traffic – 'Na LON 12/03' for instance, or 'Li BER 21/08', or 'Al MAD 07/05', but had supposed these to be weakly coded instructions to buy or sell, well, this or that commodity on this or that exchange on this or that date. We had focused our efforts on more promising leads. But the sure knowledge that these movements refer to *people* – and that Hydrogen and Helium symbolise Armand and Adolphine – we have only to crunch the itineraries of the great and good, of business people, civil servants, politicians, philanthropists – and it's a mathematical certainty that we'll hit correlations and candidates. No doubt the identities of these New Nazis will drop out like the x and the y in a quadratic equation. Indeed, Cheltenham has a team dedicated to the task 24-7."

"I nearly got myself killed, Uncle Charles."

"In that *nearly*, Louise, lies the special secret ingredient kneaded deep into every successful agent."

I could not help but feeling, fearing, that that *nearly* owed nearly nothing to *my* blonde bumbling.

"And I'm afraid, Louise, that I must urge you to lie low for at least the next few weeks."

"*Uncle Charles?*"

"You see, your colleague *chaiwallahs* at the Villa de Leny – Michelle Deneuve and Jessica Jenkins – were both so profoundly perturbed by your dramatic disappearance that they quit their shifts and scurried to divulge your entire escapade to the local Gendarmerie who, as I understand it, lost little time in initiating an investigation and raiding the place. They discovered Bald Thug dead on the spot where shot, and pitiable Perruche suffering unspeakable torments astride the Spanish Horse."

"Poor Perruche! And Madame?"

"Vanished, I fear, along with any evidence of ludicrous Blackshort buffoons."

"Perruche set me free, Uncle Charles. The French Police *do* know that?"

Momentarily, the commander wavered, wandered, caught in a crossfire of conflicted thoughts. "The young woman you knew as Perruche is in fact Angharad Conwyl, a native of Aberhaf in South Wales who disappeared, presumed abducted, while on a family holiday near Koksijde on the Flanders Coast. That was back in 1996 when she was just sixteen years old. It transpires that all these years she has been enslaved and brutalised by that monster Madame, until her very identity was forgotten to her, and even her means of speech entirely escaped her. That was, until one night last week when she opened the servants' entrance of the Villa de Leny and heard her compatriot, Jessica Jenkins, speak."

"Jessica's lilty lingo aroused and awakened Angharad's awareness of her previous self?"

"Precisely. No doubt you'll be delighted to learn that, under psychiatric care, Angharad is recovering with astounding rigour. But Madame…Madame remains a menace. Nobody knows where she'll break through the waves. So you absolutely have to stay in harbour, she has your recognition silhouette."

"Uncle Charles, are you hopeful of hunting her to surface?"

"My dear Louise, we don't even know where to start. We don't even know where she's from. The good folk of Sainte-Modeste thought *le Nord*, but Michelle Deneuve – a Parisienne – insists Madame's accent isn't French. Her best guess is that the bitch is Dutch – or English."

"Old Reverend Richards ran the Cadhurst Twinning Association for decades," Helen ventured. "The villagers of Saint-Xavier-sur-Somme used to joke that his French held a heavy Dutch twang."

"Madame flung a phrase at me in German," I rejoined. "When she had me in jankers in that ballet barre hellhole. But it didn't ring quite right. I genuinely felt she was French."

"Then you perceive our predicament," resumed the commander. "In desperation, we've decided to align our sights on the super-yacht *Bonquonne*, presently moored in the Sicilian port of Vigorno, awaiting repairs to her bow. Do you recall those dreadful drownings in the Strait of Messina, the morning that migrant ship sank? The Sunday you were staying in Sainte-Modeste?"

"Hell, yes. That was awful."

"The Italian frigate *Giuseppe Verdi* was patrolling the southernmost approaches to the Strait, monitoring the migrants' progress. Her captain insists the *Bonquonne* struck the migrants amidships."

I'm seldom speechless, but I agonised anaesthetised by

this incomprehensible intelligence.

"And the *Bonquonne*, it transpires, is registered to a Bongolian subsidiary of a Gabriel Island company of which the principal shareholders are…trusts controlled by Armand and Adolphine Lebrun. Trusts brimming with euros fraudulently filched from the investment portfolios of Merde SA."

"Then…"

"…their diabolical doctrine is not mere rancour and rhetoric."

A saddened, sullen silence ensued, as if we each, reflective, offered orisons for those drowned in the Davy-deep, for their desires, their dreams, their loves, their laughter, washed beneath the waves.

"And to cut a long tale short, the *Bonquonne* is advertising for a masseuse. To join her crew. We're scouring the service for someone with the requisite skills. If only we could get an agent on board…"

"Oh, Uncle Charles! Pick *me*! I'm a qualified masseuse! I'd love to unmask Madame! Oh, pick *me*!"

"A masseuse?" questioned Helen, incredulously. "You're making it up?"

"I am *not*! I've been one for *years*! Ever since slimeball Giles dumped me for Miss Pixie Boots. Oh, the humiliation was horrible! Ugh, day after day, face to face with their sickening smooching, the whole team at Melusine Plastics smirking and sniggering behind my back, ohh! So I set my sights on escaping to sea, serving as a masseuse on a cruise ship. I'd just got my NVQ through night school, when—"

"Along came Miles! I remember now! You soon dropped your anchor! Among other things."

"Uncle Charles, *please*! With my hair dyed black and my face full of slap they'd *never* recognise me!"

"My dear Louise, it's much too dangerous. Believe me, they'd kill you if they caught you."

I know when no means no. My dispirited, rejected, faraway gaze alighted idly onto my wristwatch. "Shit! I'm meant to be at Mother's! She keeps trying to give me my cats back!"

"Cats?"

"Jessica and Leonora. She's had them since the spring. Gwynfor's a menace with cats. He ran a roller over Leonora's tail once, it cost me a fortune in vet's fees. Crumbs, those cats are so much safer with Mother. But I haven't a half-hope in hell of honey-talking her into keeping them any longer if I'm late."

"Well, well, well, if you really must poop our party, we'll carry on plotting and planning without you."

"I must, Uncle Charles, I'm sorry. I truly must."

"Then for now we'll say cheery-bye. Oh, it very nearly slipped my mind!"

From his jacket pocket Uncle Charles handed me a cheapy cheesy black plastic mobile phone.

"It's a Pennypincher Pay-as-you-Go. Topped with a hundred pounds of call credit, programmed with a single emergency number. Call it, anytime you're endangered, day or night. Charmian or I will answer."

"A Pay-as-you-Go?"

"There's plenty of place for low-tech within our profession, Louise. Any electronic communication is infinitely prone to interception, all internet devices to infiltration and interrogation. But a simple, succinct, one-to-one call between two randomly purchased cellular telephones whose SIM cards are afterwards destroyed? It's perfectly unpredictable and therefore, practically undetectable."

I cast a glance doubtfully down at my plastic Pay-as-you-Go lifeline, identical to the one with which Tiggi had telephoned Charmian from Dirty Dave's bachelor shag pad. Something, something, something wrong was gnawing and nagging away at me, like a long-locked childhood remembrance.

"Helen," I snapped.

"Yes?"

"Hugo. Go ahead and arrange it."

And without a further word I wound my way across the evening greensward, accompanied by an ambling procession of lengthening Lowry-like shadows trudging torpid towards the gravelly car park.

2

Q x P

As I hastened my way to meet Mother, I brimmed and bubbled and boiled in tangled confusion. Something somewhere was amiss, awry. Something somewhere was wildly wrong, but what? What?

I sneaked a short cut past a bottle-brown, yellow-lettered 'Staff Only' sign, sentry to an unbecoming, uninviting woodland walk, snipping ten precious minutes from my perambulations. As I slipped into that netherworld, ebullient borders gave ground to foreboding treescape, sonorous coo fled from raucous caw, dusky sun made way for dingy shade, autumnal warmth succumbed to wintery chill.

Then, in what had seemed a deserted, desolate wood,

frighteningly quite close by, a womanly warble in mocking, mincing, melodic tones cuckooed out:

"The price will quite un-do-o-o-o-o me
Gos-sip Joan!"

Helen? No, it wasn't her song. Uncle Charles faking falsetto? No, it wasn't his style. I spun through one-eighty, expecting to see some St Lucy's Old Girl out to castigate and calumniate me for my bonne chance with EuroScoop. Instead, a brazenly beautiful thirty-something with cold silver-blonde lob, callous grey-blue eyes, and cruel thin-lip pout stood there damning and defying me, hands on hips. Armoured in amber padded anorak, olive sports leggings, and black running shoes, her feline-feminine svelteness mingling with nearly manly muscularity were instantly, instinctively intimidatory.

"Louise Fawley," she slowly, slyly insinuated, as if 'Louise Fawley' defined a depraved criminality.

My throat tightened and parched. Involuntarily, I gulped down my guilty as charged.

"I would recognise your *grosses fesses* in any place. Let me think, the last time I saw them, you were working...*oui*, as a waitress at the Villa de Leny. As I recall, you ad made to fall a tray of crème brûlées."

"*Excuse* me?" I bluffed and blustered. "I-I don't know what you're talking about."

"*Mais à ce moment-là*, unless I mistake myself, you call your name? *Ah, oui*! Jessica Jenkins!"

"I-I've possibly got a double?" I proffered in pretence.

"*Et naturellement*, I do not forget our drunken

conversation in the Bar Napoléon. *Oui*...you bent over to recoup your cigarette lighter. You wore an ideous acid green dress with your, *eh*, panty lines *ooh là là*...and you call yourself, *eh, comme pour dire*...Paula Godwin!"

"Honestly," I begged, bewildered, "you must be confusing me with someone else!"

"The games of the infants are *finis*, Mademoiselle Fawley. Permit me to present myself. I call myself Adolphine Lebrun."

Suddenly I seemed a shabby shambles in my baggy beige jumper and good-girl cream jeans. Adolphine's pristinely and perfectly toned and tuned body doubtless could outrun me, out-wrestle me, out-thump me. I felt like a fearful fly before a smugly sinister spider. I didn't dare awaken aid from my Pennypincher panic-phone. Instead, petrified, practically pooping, I shrunk and awaited my fate.

"Your efforts *irritant et d'amateur* to make infiltrate our organisation ave incommoded us ugely. The Villa de Leny, Léonard et Lionel will now rent to their cousin, your former employer, whose wife as the *polyarthrite rhumatoïde*. Our *Agent Carbone* e as an ole in is ead *parce que* your *petite amie* she as shot im. *Ma chère* Madame she dare not leave er ouse for fear she will ave an ole in er ead."

"I'm sorry about Agent Carbon," I conceded, blandly.

"Louise, join us. Replace *Agent Carbone*. Your *adoration* for the *culture* of Europe is known to us – er *arts* and er *artistes*, er *musique* and er *musiciens*, er writings and er writers. It is *impossible* for you to be *insensible* to the fate of our *continent* and our *civilisation*, to *ignorer* the *danger* from – ow does my brother say – the flotsam and the jetsam of *humanité* washed up with every tide upon our shores. Louise, you ave shown yourself a *personne ingénieuse* and *courageuse*. If you please, join our cause!"

Secretly seething, I repressed my instinct to rant and rage at her abhorrent doctrine. Cordially she had asked me to rally to her repugnant rag. Cordially I'd simply say no, hoisting high my evangelising ensign.

Mysteriously, my mind drifted downstream to dreary days long gone, to Scripture class with Sister Sapphira, to one wet Wednesday when inspired and inflamed, that meekly, mildly unassuming nun had delivered an address as might have made martyrs of any and all with ears to hear. *"Do not worry about how you will defend yourselves or what you will say, for the Holy Spirit will teach you at that time what you should say."* Every meagre morsel of enlightenment scoured and scavenged and scrounged from stuff books I now mustered to my aid, my every recollection of Cluny and Chartres, of Assisi and Urbino, of Michelangelo and Leonardo, of Erasmus and Montaigne, of Vermeer and Versailles, of Handel and Haydn, of Byron and Brunel, of Renoir and Rutherford, of all that which, albeit unbeknown to us, makes us, us. I, stuttering, stammering, panicking, palpitating, bravely began.

"Adolphine, all cultures must source from somewhere streams of ever-rejuvenating creative, artistic or inspirational impulses, if those cultures are not to scorch and wither and parch like under-nourished potted plants. The wisdom, strength and beauty of European culture from age to age have been founded on its infinite ability to appropriate and assimilate a rainbow of ideas and influences and fashions and flavours from every continent and creed. For Europe to bar its gates against people from distant lands would be for Europe to make outcasts and outlaws of its own cultural posterity."

With which, I'd stumped myself into silence. Seldom had I ever said anything so seemingly intelligent.

Adolphine stretched to a sickly, insipid smile. "*Eh, bien*. I comprehend *complètement*. We must, as say the English, agree to disagree, *je pense*. My brother e will be *très désappointé. Eh, c'est la vie.*"

"And now, if you'll excuse me, I have to take care of my cats." And with thunderous thoughts I turned and resumed my retreat. *Join* them? *Join* them? My *arse*!

"*Au revoir, Mademoiselle Fawley!*" bade Adolphine, in menacing, malevolent, death-knell notes.

A sudden, swinging, stinging, smash to my skull… anguishing, agonising, dizzying, darkening…falling, falling, through inter-stellar blackness…a thudding thumping…then earthy, leafy autumnal scents…

3

If Memory Serves

The Melusine Plastics Pussy Posse were out on the town, out to have fun, out to do harm, our high heels clicking, clacking on kerbstones, our slender legs barely braving the Christmas chill, our bum-skimming skimp-skirts man-magnets for every greedy gaze as we chattered and cackled with gaudy gaiety our prick-tease ways along alleys thick with curry-sauce chip-shops, past dismal-dark piss-pong doorways, to the tempo of thud-thud badass bass from jukebox-junkie beer-breath pubs and clubs.

Tracey was out to get trolleyed; Lucy was out to get laid; Stacey was out to get Kayleigh laid. Kayleigh lived for the love of her life, her mobile phone, pushed into her poodle perm. Amid girl-chat and traffic-growl and season-to-be-jolly, she strode strenuously ahead, oblivious to our clamorous catcalls:

"Kayleigh! We're heading for *Romero's*! KAYLEIGH!"

A sliver of silver cut my darkness like a zigzag of luminescent lightning.

"Kayleigh? Wake up, love! Kayleigh?"

Gently, gradually, my mind morphed into the here and now, into the sunshine searing and stinging at my tight eyelids, into the softness and snugness of my slumbering surroundings, into the encouraging, enticing, tranquil tones beckoning me back from my brink.

"Kayleigh? Come on, love! Kayleigh?"

My eyes gazed upon a goddess, her tangled, tousled mess and mass of chocolatey-auburn locks and dreadlocks cascading about her burnished, bronzed, beauteous visage, her thick black eyebrows arching, arcing above her gentle emerald eyes luscious with lashes bejazzled with gems of oranges, yellows, scarlets; her rich lips glistening pinky-copper, a dainty golden ring bejewelling her cute nose.

"Kayleigh!" My delectable deity bestowed a benign smile. "Oh, thank heaven you've come to!"

Still semi-senseless, scarcely aware of my whereabouts, my eyes alighted upon the pretty pink plastic name badge labelling my Nightingale, fixed to her trim, taut beauty tunic of transfiguration white:

KYLIE – BEAUTICIAN

And in that instant, my confusion and consternation mounting and maddening, with peripheral vision I sensed

my own chocolatey bob, my own white-as-snow tunic, my own little pretty pink name badge:
KAYLEIGH – MASSEUSE

I jolted bolt upright. A bewildering, beguiling apparition stared, scared, straight at me. Her hot-chocolate tresses tossing wayward about her copper-tone face, her deep, dark eyebrows gracing her long-lash eyes, her gawping, gasping lips hanging heavy with pouting bronze, a gypsy ring of gold adorning her snub-like nose. Me, and yet, not me. Mine was the face I knew more assuredly than all others, but this me I'd never known. Me as might have been me, had I been a sort of sexy sort of girl.

"Relax, love," soothed Kylie, in softly, kindly, tones. "Don't fret yourself. You're on the *Bonquonne*."

Aboard the *BONQUONNE*? What? My muddled, muddied mind catapulted back through my time-and-space blackness to Hexhurst Gardens; to that semi-somnolent fat satsuma sun, melting like marmalade over skyscape and treescape; to those flavoursome, savoursome sausages-with-chutney; to Uncle Charles' crack-brain plan to smuggle me stowaway onto the *Bonquonne*, disguised as a masseuse; to Adolphine's depraved invitation to enlist in her obnoxious organisation. OHH! Wasn't it *OBVIOUS*? Those noisome Nazis had totally turned the tables on MI69! Yes, as the commander had connived, I'd boarded the *Bonquonne* as the ship's masseuse; but not in the guise of a spy, in the chains of a slave!

"Kylie!" I pleaded, panted, a stomach-sickening sobbing retching me, racking me, ransacking me. "My name isn't

Kayleigh. It's Louise! I've been kidnapped! Shanghaied! I've got to get off here!"

"Oh, I can *promise* you, you'll get off here," teased Kylie, goading and glinting. "Every single night if you feel like. Nobody goes without on board the *Bonquonne*."

In disbelief, in denial, dizzily my eyes swept my surroundings. Yes, a cabin…sunshine cascaded across like super-trouper beams from two tiny portholes. Yes, Kylie's and Kayleigh's cabin, a twin cabin, its dreamy divans plumped with snowy duck-down duvets. Outside, on pantomime cue, some tug or other sounded a chortling toot, while seagulls, squealing, pealing, circled in clamorous mad madrigal.

"Besides, you've picked a perfect day for't join't crew," encouraged Kylie, her Lancastrian accent growing more marked. "Tonight's our last night in't port, our bow's patched up. We'll be makin way for Cyprus in't mornin. There's a party this evenin, all ands. It'll be a great laugh. We've got an Indian dance troupe comin n all sorts. Oh, you'll love life on't *Bonquonne*. Oh, Kayleigh! Please stay!"

I puzzled perplexed by Kylie's dreamy, dopey features, by her sleepiest, serenest of smiles, by her two huge emerald eyes. Through her thick mask of maquillage, a familiar face formed before my gaze.

Joanne! Joanne's missing sister! Her beautician sister! Oh, her name! What was her name?

"Laura?" I tentatively ventured. "Is it Laura?"

An evil demon seemingly wound around, searing and screaming, wincing and weeping through Laura's tortured soul. In painful, tearful tones, eyes tight and head hung, she uttered in guttural groans, "Kayleigh, there is no Laura. Kayleigh, there is no Louise. We're Kylie and Kayleigh now."

"But Joanne has never given up on you," I persisted, poignantly. "She's never left Sainte-Modeste."

"Louise, love, there's no escape. Blank your past. Forget Louise. Be Kayleigh. Be Kayleigh, n *LIVE*!"

My life seemed set to implode, imprisoned as a pristinely painted and preened, pedicured and manicured, mannequin masseuse. I hardly heeded as Kylie narrated the fate of Naomi, my pining predecessor who, one fortnight before, had fled in the dead of the night. Moments following the farewell click of the cabin door, a squeal, a shot, a splosh, then sickening stillness. As I slipped softly, silently into my netherworld, a world of chaotic, kaleidoscopic, phantasmal scenes and sounds, I sought a lifeline of normality in the garish artwork chromium-framed before me. A face, a human face, a face of splodges and splashes of oranges and greens and purples and greys, a face unlike a face, a face so like a face, undefined yet penetrating, penetrating to personality, like a lover poking and prodding inexorably to orgasm, this artist had mercilessly, magnificently brought forth unconditional truth, subjugating their sitter in climactic surrender with the flicks and twists of an omniscient brush.

"Kayleigh? You're driftin off again, love! KAYLEIGH!"

4

Chameleon

The life of a ship's masseuse was far from deadly dull. After enduring the blithesome blunderings of Uncle Charles and his puerile Project Godiva, with champagne euphoria my ever-awakening horizons dawned and dawned before me like endless sparkling sea after endless sparkling sea, sunshine-shimmering with shoals of wassail-wild piratical parties and lots of rock-hard jolly rogerings.

Kayleigh I pressed into service that same afternoon. Surrendering myself to her skills, permitting those heavenly, heavily scented aromatherapeutic oils to gently gladden and deaden my bamboozled brain, deeply, dreamily, inhaling the intoxicating aromatic amnesiac, performing my arts as if in a Delphic trance, building and building through firmer and firmer effleurage to hacking and cupping and patting and slapping; then down, down, diminishing my pressure and passion to a sleepy, smiley finale.

First, at 13:00 hours, came garrulous Giorgio, head chef, pining, panging, longing for his apple-eye grandchildren; enthusing, effusing, gabbling about his moreish morsels, spicy sweetmeats in honour of our Indian dancers; sincerely, promising to slake my homesickness with pies and pastries *inglese*. Second, at 14:00 hours, came taciturn Tatyana, chief of security; moodily, morosely, mourning her frozen motherland; curtly, crossly, instructing me which decks on *Bonquonne* were out of bounds to me; slyly, pledging to procure me any crazy cacophony of deadhead drugs I desired. Third, at 15:00 hours, came randy Rima, entertainments manager; tantalising, titillating, with tales of males squeezed and pleased in supine subjugation; excitedly, expectantly, thrilling away the hours until her Indian dance troupe spectacular; indulgently, intimating her secret shortlist of guys on board who would.

To find oneself incarcerated, yet liberated, to feel oneself humiliated, yet exhilarated, yes, Kayleigh was the merest menial aboard *Bonquonne*, earning her bread and bed with the skills her hands had practised and perfected, those antediluvian ten-digit tools our scratchy-arsey monkey ancestors had borne from birth, chattering and jabbering their ascent from jungle to savannah. Yet, Kayleigh was free. Freed from the fortress walls gavelled and chiselled to enclose Louise and her multi-millions; saved from the earthly damnation of tongue-lashing, nit-picking, eternal maternal disapprobation; spared from the frog-snogging next-please dinner-date nightmare known as husband-hunting.

I smiled to myself to wonder what Sarah Scobie of the *Southampton Star* might make of my demise. "The mysterious disappearance from Hexhurst Gardens of EuroScoop millionairess Louise Fawley…"

Instead, Kylie and Kayleigh slowly surmounted the stunning see-through spiral staircase amidships, that wrought-iron wormhole to the elegance and decadence of Main Deck, whose walls glistened and gleamed with sumptuous teak inlaid with stylistic cartoons of lovers entwined exotic and erotic in creams and beiges and browns, where silver space-age sofas suggested imminent alien abduction.

Like a pair of irrepressible, irresponsible schoolgirls, over-eagerly, over-excitedly, we homed like pigeons towards the hotbed hubbub emanating aft. Rapidly our air-conditioned comfort surrendered to sizzling Sicilian scorch, and I sighed, relieved that I'd acquiesced in Kylie's choice of long, light, short-sleeved blouses patchworked in crazy arrays of hues and styles – purples, reds, oranges, yellows in florals, paisleys, polka dots, tartans – almost hiding our gloss-black boy-short big-bum bikini bottoms.

The atmosphere pervading and perfuming the party was carnival. Elatedly, Giorgio revelled in his bhajis and pakoras and chakulis, delighting in sharing his surprises with an appreciative audience. Elegantly, Rima swanned, touchy-greety everywhere but stoppy-chatty nowhere.

Elusively, Tatyana scanned and scrutinised incessantly, her icy iron eyes locked and loaded. Meanwhile, in threes and fours the electric-ecstatic crew, whether on duty in East-of-Suez whites, the men promoting their biceps, the women parading their thighs; whether off-duty in Hawaiian dazzle, the guys gesticulating beautiful game, the gals chattering handbags and gladrags; all alike bubbled with expectations.

The port and town of Vigorno provided a picturesque-perfect theatrical backdrop for our evening's entertainment. A Baroque extravaganza of exquisite creamy-ivory cathedral-like churches amid crazy conglomerations of higgledy-piggledy houses, all seemingly sculpted from an iridescent icing-sugar, all somehow sighing with the weary weight of centuries, as if the whole town would slowly slip, melt, mingle with the Mediterranean. Above, a serenely silvery supermoon basked the buildings in a luminescent light, as the darkness-deepening evening sky displayed in over-arching palette its blues from turquoise west to midnight east. The town's gentle reflections softly shimmered so invitingly, so enticingly, in the so-black, sloe-black inky calm, that I fancied Salacia and Venilia might mischievously raise an autumnal storm to wrench Vigorno from dry land and present it to their watery lord.

My mind meandered back through space and time to a dank, damp, stuffy, stinky, custard-and-cream classroom, lair of Miss Bogg and her dreary Latin lessons. Involuntarily, inconceivably, I mouthed mechanically an Ode of Horace long forgotten, its sudden relevance resonating, reverberating, urging:

Do not presume, it's sacrilege, for you or I to know
What fates the gods have granted us, Leuconoe, nor should we seek to read
Our fortunes in the stars. Oh better by far, 'whatever will be, will be',
Whether Jove allots more winters, or else this is the last
When waves will senseless dash themselves against the pumice shores.

With a jump, a jolt, shocked I sensed Adolphine at my side. In surprisingly comforting, caressing tones, she whispered the Ode's concluding couplet, pressing a glass of ruby red liquid into my yielding hand.

Be content, enjoy your wine, and, as life is short, cut short your dreams to fit.
Even as we speak, time covetous flies: seize each day, for tomorrow never comes.

Adolphine's silvery-blonde lob glowed ghostly in the argentine moonlight, her steely grey-blue eyes, her stony, slender pout conflicting with her softening, soothing demeanour.

"You see, Kayleigh, you and I, we are not so very *différent*," she coaxed and cajoled. "And of course, you may become again Louise in any moment you choose. *Simplement, remplacez Agent Carbone.*"

Though I plumbed the depths, I sounded out no suitable response, neither lurking in head nor in heart.

"What's the poison?" I proffered at last, gauchely.

"Ahh, the Raspberry Brainfucker, our ouse cocktail! Ohh, *Mon Dieu*! Take *le jus de framboise, le Martini, le qu'est-que ç'est*…only Giorgio, only e knows ow. *Mais, mwah*! You will love!"

Adolphine greedily gulped and guzzled, downing her drink.

"Louise," she resumed, the moistening, mellowing Martini loosening her lips, "you ave not need to believe the bullshit of my brother. You think I admire im? Follow im? *Merde! Mais, demandez-vous*…ow much would I gain each year as instructress of fitness? *Pouah! Mais…à bord du Bonquonne*, I ave the lifestyles and the luxuries of a princess."

I moistened my lips with Raspberry Brainfucker. Mmm…enticingly, entreatingly, irresistibly delicious!

"*Et aussi*, the brute my brother as in is mind to be *Agent Carbone*, e is…*le cochon*. *Oh là là*, when at the Villa de Leny my brother e is making is speech *pompeux* and you make to fall the *crème brûlées*, I fear the death of laugh! *Ohh, je vous en prie*, Louise, be *Agent Carbone*! Be *ma femme de droite*!"

Before I could so much as strain my brain to contemplate or comprehend Adolphine's bizarre proposal, above and behind us light and life and laughter burst forth, heralding a tumult and torrent of silken saris in emerald and mustard and cobalt and tangerine and olive and crimson, as six Indian dancers, greeting the crowd with serene smiles and winsome waves, cascaded the steps from upper deck to their makeshift stage at the stern. Welcoming whoops ticker-taped their gay perambulations to a hitherto unheeded canvas depicting a mandir in idyllic tranquillity, while the hypnotic, narcotic, joyful, jubilant rhythms of traditional Indian music pervaded and perfumed the evening air.

As the dancers eased into their enchanting, entrancing spectacle, the heady, heavenly, harmonies of Indian singers intensified the musical, lyrical fragrance. I'd been a ballerina, but my mind totally tangled trying to interpret the dancers' sinuous, sensual, swirling, snake-like lines. Incongruously, red-lit surtitles spanned the space above the brushwork mandir. Awed and appreciative, I followed them.

My Love is like the Snow Leopard, stealthy and sure-footed.
He pounces the crags and crevices, stalking his helpless prey.
With dread and delight I await my fate; I know no escape, and desire none.
My Love is like the Snow Leopard, stealthy and sure-footed.

The music jaunted, jangled; the dancers gyrated, gesticulated; the singers warbled, wailed; the whole melted me, mellowed me. Momentarily alone, serenely I sipped my Raspberry Brainfucker down, down, tingling my taste buds, and my situation suddenly struck me as sensational – to become *Agent Carbone*, swanking it on the bridge, strutting it on the decks, spitting orders at my cowed crew in my kinky, kooky, white-as-white, bitch-on-board, sexy, sex-me, uniform.

As Adolphine approached, grasping two glass goblets brimming with Raspberry Brainfucker, her harsh visage happily honeyed into heavenly. Casually carefree in her boat-bum attire of Breton sweater, navy shorts and brown ankle boots, she seemed as relaxed and contentedly commonplace as any girl, in any bar, in any port, the whole wide Mediterranean around.

"Ohh, Louise! *Ma chère amie*! *Vous avez décidé*? You will join us, *oui*? You will be our *Agent Carbone*?"

That magnificent moon, serenely silvery still, shone ominously over the somnolent squares and streets of crumbling Vigorno; alike on insignificant me. The seaside suburbs were oh-so teasingly, tantalisingly proximate that yowling, howling dogs sometimes yelped all too audible above the jubilant Indian jamboree. Yes, town was just north of my own peculiar Mason-Dixon Line, but the 250 yards to town might just as well have been the 250 million miles to the Moon.

Practically punch-drunk with enraged and embattled emotions, inwardly writhing, wrestling, wrangling, I shuddered with bitter distaste and disgust to imagine myself as a *collaborateur*. But if I suffered myself to be battened below on lower deck as a massage-monkey, what could I possibly detect or discover to disclose to Uncle Charles? Whereas, as Adolphine's companion and confidante, as Adolphine's favourite and friend, doubtless there would be secrets to steal, lots and lots to learn.

"Adolphine," I capitulated, wrapping my suppliant arms around her, "of *course* I'll be *Agent Carbone*!"

"Ohh, Louise!" Adolphine exulted. "This is an appy evening, *oui*? These are the news *merveilleuse*!"

And holding my head between her hands, she sealed

our deal by branding each of my cheeks with a lingering kiss, and a telltale tingling started to spangle inside me. Oh, *please*! Not *Adolphine*!

5

DE PROFUNDIS

I pushed and prized myself away to gaze empty-headed over party deck, through the lissom-limbed disco-dance revelry to the effervescent energy of the irrepressible, indefatigable Indian dancers. Their hypnotising, mesmerising rhythms blending with sonorous soul-migrating song sped me elsewhere, somewhere; on my own magic-carpet adventure above Mughal minarets and parapets to meet my maharaja, my lavish lover, mannerly, manly, masterly; unquenchably wealthy, unimpeachably kingly.

Then slowly I sensed that one of the dancers, the plumpest dancer, the dancer in the tangerine sari, had fixed, even fixated, her puzzled, perturbed rangefinder eyes onto me and stared, bewildered and bewitched, as if she alone could discern and define the me behind the make-up.

It was Charmian Mudher!

Instantly, as if with a flick of a switch, the mellow, magnificent mandir and gorgeous, gyrating dancers merged into murky, gloomy gloaming. Soul-searching songs and madly meditative melodies were silenced. On disco deck, grumbles and groans buzzed like bees in a stinging, swarming, angry mass.

"Oh, a power cut! Typical. A power cut! Wouldn't you know it? A power cut! Just getting going – a power cut!"

And just as suddenly, blinding white lights beamed super-trouper from the dockside, the dance troupe bristled with pistols, like a Scots schiltrom's spears and, in their midst, with crackling hand-held tannoy, in impeccable dark-navy pinstriped three-piece, towered Commander Charles Chumleigh.

"I hold an Interplod Gold Notice requiring the arrest and extradition of Mademoiselle Adolphine Eva Lebrun on suspicion of the criminal abduction and false incarceration of Miss Louise Paula Fawley."

Tatyana sought to secretly sneak her pistol from her shorts pocket. Instead, a twitch from Charmian's arm, the singing sound of a shot and Tatyana's hand oozed blood, her pistol clattering down onto the deck.

"*Сука!*" she squeaked, nursing her hurting hand between her bloodening thighs.

And then, from behind either end of a long, low, old stone quayside warehouse, growled two huge dark khaki six-wheeled armoured cars, their swivel-gunners toting and training their shoot-to-shreds weapons onto the stunned and silenced *Bonquonne*. Each was flanked by two trotting lines of hunky, handsome Italian infantry in burgundy berets and camouflage combats, all with badass black machine guns at clutch-to-kill. Finally, a *toot, toot* signalled through the gathering evening greyness a bright white craft of the Guardia Costiera rounding the western breakwater, sealing the seas from retreat.

Adolphine, squirming and shaking, seized me by my biceps.

"*Louise!*" she pleaded, delirious with despair. "*Eh, échappons-nous, sur les jet skis! Vite, vite!*"

"No, Adolphine!" I sought to soothe. "It's all over! Stay! I'll let them know you meant me no harm!"

"*NON!*" she howled, in hysterical hell. "*Je ne veux pas passer ma vie en prison! Laisse-moi libre! Vous ne savez pas ce que j'ai fait!*"

We held one another hard by the arms, grappling and grasping to gain a grip, but our see-saw scrum saw my flip-flop feet flail and fail against Adolphine's chunky, clumpy ankle boots. Viciously, Adolphine angrily stamped at my naked toes. Next I felt myself toppling, tumbling, backwards, downwards, clinging to squealing, screaming Adolphine. Then falling, falling, sensing the creamy-white side of *Bonquonne* as, scrapping still, we sploshed and spluttered down, down into the chilly, clammy, smelly, salty, dead-dark, lead-limbed, dead-deep, daren't-breathe, turgid, torrid, aquatic panic of underwater.

The condemned confounded, committed, consumed; call me, count me, among the beauteous blessed.

A glimmer, a shimmer, a glimpse, a shaft of brighter, lighter, then euphoric, ecstatic, splashing emancipation from the disorientating, debilitating serfdom of the seas. With a whoosh, like Ahab's white whale, I broke surface amid the zigzag dazzle-dance of frantic, frenetic search beams. Blinded, a crazy clamorous chaos of cheers cascaded my ears with, "She's there! *Lei è lì! Elle est là! Ze is daar!*"

Behind me the grumbly groan of an outboard motor moaned closer. I, choking and coughing, spitting and snotting, devoid of dignity, suffered two spinach-savouring sailors to heave-ho haul me over the rough rigid-rubber hull of their inflatable dinghy, only for those rescuers to explode into ribaldrous laughter.

"*Ah, bellissima bambina! Ah, culo carino! Ah, bellissima bambina!*"

Intuitively, instinctively, sensing shame, I placed my palms on my upturned buttocks and detected a dreaded faux pas: Neptune had nabbed my bikini bottoms! Suddenly, with a dull thud a bundled-up Union Jack fell in front of my face, as Kylie's Lancastrian twang catcalled across the crackling tannoy:

"Ahoy, Kayleigh! Cover your fat backside with that. You're shameless!"

Gratefully, graciously, I wrapped that tattered flag around my middle and stood, slowly, shakily, to an amphitheatric crescendo of cheering and clapping and whooping and whistling alike from shipside and dockside, from soldier and sailor, from Indian and Italian. And in their midst, beaming benignly like the proudest parent, triumphed my Uncle Charles, honouring me with the sweetest of salutes.

6

God Save Al the Rowte

The searching, sneaking chilly winds of autumn had blown open the creaking gates of summer; dancing oak leaves and ash leaves in greens and yellows and browns their wanton ways across rippling greensward, ravishing trees into gawkily awkward semi-naked states, chasing sparrows rough-and-tumble to evergreen shelters, pursuing woodpigeons deeper still deeper into thick stark copses. The saddened, slate-grey stratus skies rolled along like ragged rocks, spitting spatterings of icy showers.

We ambled alongside former fishponds, relics of toilsome monastic ages long gone, with acers in fierce and fiery scarlets and oranges and yellows hazily, half-heartedly reflected in murky, miry greeny-grey autumnal waters, and towering tree trunks stretching gaunt and gnarled into gloomy, grisly heavens.

Cosy in my purple padded anorak, comfy in my thick black tights, I had longed to linger at Hexhurst Gardens Tea Rooms for a third exquisitely delicious mint hot chocolate, crowned with clotted cream, but Uncle Charles had insisted that inclement weather was whipping in on a wild westerly wind.

"We're informed that frogmen found her curled upon the seafloor, a few fathoms from *Bonquonne*, apparently in the attitude of attempting to remove her boot. Indeed, her left bootlace was undone."

"Poor Adolphine!" I lamented, laconically. "What an agonising way to die!"

"My dearest, darlingest god-daughter, I am truly astounded at your conscience and compassion for your callous erstwhile captor. Without doubt, once those noisome New Nazis had wheedled their filching fingers into your fortune, they would have drowned *you* with a pair of stout steel-toed boots."

"Uncle Charles, I'm not so sure. I think Adolphine was simply addicted to the superyacht lifestyle and felt friendless, imprisoned, isolated. I'm *certain* she didn't believe in all her brother's Nazi nonsense."

"Well, well, well, that may be true, but her high-life hankerings drove her to indelible crimes. It was on *her* order that *Bonquonne* rammed and sank that migrant ship; per *her* own hand in the log."

A spurt of salty, stingy tears arrested me. I could scarcely cope with the notion of an evil Adolphine.

"Is there any news of Perruche, Uncle Charles? Angharad, I mean?"

"Yes. I am delighted to relate that she has confounded every pessimistic prognosis for her recovery."

"Oh, I'm so glad! Oh, I'd *love* to meet Angharad, Uncle Charles! I probably owe her my life!"

"She is quite the celebrity now in her native village. Her sister set her up on Scrapbook, and almost the entire complement of old Aberhaf Comprehensive School have befriended her, pupils and teachers alike. She keeps an extensive and energetic correspondence from her hospital bed in Nice.

"Meanwhile," continued Uncle Charles, "Joanne and Laura Murphy are back in Lancashire, and engaged in accumulating – I believe it's described as crowdfunding – to establish themselves in an English-style tea shop in Sainte-Modeste, and exhibit for sale Joanne's seascapes and townscapes."

"Ooh, good for them! I *must* pay them a visit. English cream tea on the French Riviera, irresistible!"

"By the way, I understand that you succeeded in hacking a trail through *Wines of the World*?"

"Almost, Uncle Charles. If I remember correctly, as far as, umm…Chapter 23 – Chenin and Cabernet."

"Hm. How singular then that after Agent Smith had kindly retrieved and returned for me the volume from Hôtel Louis-Philippe, I should discover a St Lucy's School bookmark wedged in at page six."

I scrunched my lips with guilt. Doh, caught out again! Fawley, you idiot!

"Damn, I'd almost forgotten! I've been carrying this blasted thing around with me for weeks!" Uncle Charles slid his black-gloved hand into a pocket of his silky silvery-grey topcoat, and withdrew a small shield-shaped brown-paper package. Unwrapped, it revealed a replica coat of arms.

"A gift for you from my old school friend, Sir Nigel Naseby – the arms of Sir John de Fawley, granted by Richard the Second in 1377 in recognition of Sir John's initiative in driving a fierce French raid from the Hampshire coast. A hind couchant gules between two stags rampant sable all on a field argent."

Ohh, a hind couchant between two stags rampant… in my dreams!

"Do you know, your man Gwynfor, when he learned that you were unaccounted for, wrapped himself up in his old duffle coat, hopped onto the last bus, up to his old regimental barracks in Godlingsbury, and hammered on the gates at next to midnight, hollering, 'It's never right, it isn't! It's never right!'"

"That certainly sounds like Gwynfor, bless him. You'll meet him, Uncle Charles. He's picking me up."

"Well, well, well, you might just find that a more charming and convivial chauffeur awaits your pleasure."

The twisting tarmac path snaked its way through a great green dismal-dark rhododendron copse, before unexpectedly ending at a vast, stark, beigey-yellowy, sand-

and-gravel car park. There, guarding my demonic, diabolic, hell-red Montvecchio Tarantella, stood Gwynfor, sentry-silent, his pale pate rotating droid-like leftwards then rightwards from within the warmth of his rich-knit oatmeal sweater.

And there, ten yards to their left, dizzily dishy Dave Lanchbury leant against his golden-metallic Bayern B2 coupé, grinning generously in bad-boy black leather bomber and pectoral-perfecting tight white T-shirt. Doubtless lurking down in those slim-fit sky-blue denims, his pleasure-purveying packet was pulsating, palpitating proudly at the prospect of spearing me a second – make that a third – time.

I faced no agonising indecision. This was a guaranteed genuine no-brainer. As I wandered winningly towards Dave, marvelling as his stiff-upper-lip grin dissolved into delighted, enlightened smiles, I knew precisely what womanly duty demanded. As Dave anticipated embrace, I donkey-kicked hard, hard, into his groin, then ran like hell pell-mell amid yelps of "Bitch!" and my own sniggering and snorting.

"Quick, Gwynfor! I'll drive! Quick, into the passenger seat!"

"Ho ho ho! Straight in the knackers! I can guess what that was for, Louise Fawley!"

With wicked wild wheelspin and scandalous six-litre roars, our tyres spitting stones and droving dustclouds, we slipped and slid through the exit gateway into Hexhurst Lane, topping the ton before we reached Beauhurst Junction. Neither of us noticed Sergeant Stan Poniard, his magnificent moustaches outmatched only by his triumphant greedy grin as, grasping his new-toy speed-gun rifle-like, he copped my 110 miles per hour and my doubtlessly dangerous driving.

Magistrate Adelina Percival relished and revelled in dishing me my seven-day sentence, declaring that a fine would be futile, and insisting prison would teach me a lesson. Oh! A moody afternoon in your own flower-filled garden can't compare with four grim grey cell walls when it comes to deadly dull!